GOTH GIRL

GOTH GIRL

Robert Shepyer

GOTH GIRL

HISTRIA
SciFi&Fantasy

Histria SciFi & Fantasy

Las Vegas ◊ Chicago ◊ Palm Beach

Published in the United States of America by
Histria Books
7181 N. Hualapai Way, Ste. 130-86
Las Vegas, NV 89166 USA
HistriaBooks.com

Histria SciFi & Fantasy is an imprint of Histria Books dedicated to outstanding books in the genres of science fiction and fantasy. Titles published under the imprints of Histria Books are distributed worldwide.

Library of Congress Control Number: 2024931086

ISBN 978-1-59211-474-0 (softbound)
ISBN 978-1-59211-483-2 (eBook)

CHAPTER ONE

There is so much pain in the world, but Alexandra lives apart from it all. Yet, for some reason, she still felt so sad. Watching her for a living, it was my job to learn as much as possible about the sorrow she kept hidden in her heart. Before I was assigned her case, I knew nothing of goth music. I expected it to sound like Gregorian chants when I first heard the name. As it would turn out, gothic music isn't much like the architecture. The only link between the two might be that Alexandra loved them both.

My whole life, I've been preparing for this job. From a very young age, I showed promise in voyeurism. I didn't play with other children, I watched them and made games out of learning their behaviors. Once I was ready to begin my higher education, I launched to the top of all my surveillance studies classes. I was a natural, superior to any specialized machine. My mind and cold heart were able to deduce how thoughts translated into actions, and more importantly, how feelings translated into thoughts. No inventor has made a machine capable of this, and it's already 2066. If robotics were supposed to become sentient, it would've already happened. No, people realized they were irreplaceable, that's why it's so important to keep them under control. Society no longer aims to replace us like it once did. Society is all about convenience in exchange for control, and both require surveillance. That's why overseeing voyeurs like myself are in high demand and low supply. Governments and private businesses hire me to watch high-profile subjects or entire populations. Alexandra was a government job, classified since birth. A uniquely American case. For all I know, they might've discovered the secret of this special girl long before she was born. I learned a little bit about her past from off-duty eavesdropping but not nearly enough; they wouldn't tell me everything. I've only been on her case coming up on two years now.

When I mentioned Alexandra lived apart from all the world's pain, I mean the world we made for her was separate from the actual world. She was a subject in a simulated reality of our creation. Everything she knew of the world outside her gothic mansion on the top of a gothic hill had been programmed to illicit her happiness. We needed to keep her happy to keep her sane, because the last thing we wanted was an unhinged Alexandra. It just so happened that the things that made most people sad made her happy. We coded the winter nights to be poetic and dreary with ritual howls and iceblink moons. We designed summer days that saw vintage cars full of nuclear families, and more roses than could possibly be plucked from nature. Anything was possible in our simulation, but in reality, she was living inside a two-story white cube in a giant white laboratory on the thirty-fifth floor of the federal building.

We set her simulation in the past. Aesthetically, everything outside her house appeared vintage. She loved the clothes and the way people's faces were shaped back then. We made her think her Los Angeles neighborhood was special in that way, held back in time. She felt lucky to live among people that appreciated antiques and old-world craftsmanship. The year of her simulation was 2020, and small reminders of this were sprinkled all over the landscape. A billboard in the distance of her window's view, sitting where the suburbs met the seedy city, would flash different advertisements every day. We would use these advertisements to inspire her daily routine and choices. The reason we told her the year was 2020 was because this was around the time in American history the new way came to be. Also, all the best goth music was released by 2020.

Alexandra's favorite musicians were immortalized in her room by one-of-a-kind art signed by the bands and artist. She loved New Order, so we got her a New Order poster painted by Damien Hirst. She loved Cold Cave, so we got her a photograph of Wesley Eisold taken by David Lynch. Lastly, the Cure — Alexandra loved the Cure. We got her a first pressing of "Disintegration," and inside the sleeve was a strand of Robert Smith's hair. We spared no expense to make her feel like her life was worth living and when I say we, I mean our team of scientists, programmers, bureaucrats, supervisors, actors, technicians, strategists, and I. Perhaps this team's most important member was Alexandra's mother, the actress playing the character of Vera Quinn. The character of Vera felt so terrible her daughter had to grow up without a father, she did everything in her power to grant every one of Alexandra's wishes. Testing determined Alexandra's emotional responses to male adults were almost always negative, even if the males were family. They would make her depressed and despondent. Men seemed to react to Alexandra oddly too. Even if they were paid to play a character that was nothing but nice to her, they felt compelled to rebel against their instructions and meet her kindness with cruelty. So, we gave her a loving mother and estranged father. We told Alexandra her father was a musician constantly on tour. We thought instilling in her the hope he may return was better than giving her no father at all. Her father's name was David; he was an Englishman. Sometimes I wondered who authored Alexandra's story, and I imagined there was some development team, spitting ideas back and forth in some dark, smokey room.

Even with all the accommodations we made, she was still depressed. We thought if we took away triggers like goth music, she would recover, but after a few days without it, she started contemplating suicide. I can't read her mind, but luckily for us, Alexandra is the biggest open book anyone could ever surveille. She blogs about everything. We gave her a large following that demands content, and she loves interacting with them, even forming relationships with a few. She hasn't realized every online follower is actually me, but even if she does, she likes me a lot, in all my incarnations. This job is a breeze for an overseeing voyeur. A monkey could do it, let alone a machine. However, Alexandra's case is so sensitive, if even the slightest discrepancy goes unnoticed, the results could be catastrophic. All that said, I don't do this job for the money, the challenge, or even so I can say I was hired to watch one of the most important human beings in the species' history. I do this job because I love her. What else would you expect? I spend my life so close but so far from her every hour of every day, the distance only makes my heart grow fonder. I'm the one person who recognizes her beauty and sees her pain. Maybe it's sick, but it's still love.

***

I finish my work after Alexandra goes to sleep and start it before she wakes up. She often stirs awake between those two points, so I have Sylvia work the graveyard shift. Sylvia observed Alexandra before the government hired me full time. As tireless as her eyes are, they're untrained to look for the right clues to report. She comes from an older school of voyeurism, which is flawed on a theoretical level. Sylvia is tall, slender, about forty years old, has beautiful, long, silver hair, dresses in a style one might call "alternative business," is English, and rarely speaks to me. From what I understand, she never speaks to anyone at work, making the late shift perfect for her.

After my shift, it takes me five minutes to get home from the federal building. It rarely rains in this city, but it is pouring tonight. When I get to my apartment, Hobbes is there to greet me, nuzzling up against my ankle. He stays so cold during the day, seeing his friend Ovid is his one chance to warm up for the night. Hobbes is my penguin. Ovid is me. I wasn't born with that name. Ovid is short for overseeing voyeur. Every authority figure I've ever worked for calls me that, so it stuck. My parents named me Johnny. My apartment is small, cold, and gray. I imagine Alexandra would like it. She would find the space rather inspiring. Somewhere a hermetic hunchback would find sanctuary.

I want to watch the news, so I flex the right neuron to send the thought into my Mind Tap and turn it on. Channel Zero projects onto my wall as Hobbes and I cozy up on my couch. I grip at the air toward a can of beer in the distance, and it floats into my hand. Hobbes does the same with his wing. We crack open our ice-cold beers and we're getting buzzed tonight.

"Should I order us a pizza?" I ask Hobbes.

Hobbes nods and takes a long swig.

With a simple thought, my Mind Tap orders us a large pizza with extra anchovies. The sound of a cash register's ring echoes through my skull as a cool ten dollars is taken from my account.

"Tonight, a group of anarchist imbeciles died in the streets," the news anchor happily begins.

"Who's going to clean them up? Not the mayor, I bet," I say, spitting a hot take.

The news I watched was customized for me. Not a single headline running across the ticker would ever challenge a single one of my inclinations. There was never an opinion shared that I didn't hold. It was my favorite show. This was one feature that made the Mind Tap such revolutionary tech, it meant people didn't have to share reality with each other anymore, they could have one all their own. Because she was a staunch leftist, Alexandra would be disgusted by my political views. In our time, she would be considered a centrist. Meanwhile, I was a conservative, or in her timeframe, an asshole. If she knew what direction the world took after 2020, she would move so far left she'd fall off a cliff. This is how most artists are. Liberal to the bone. Everything goes. God first, out the window. How else does one liberate? Whenever I saw Alexandra posting about politics, I became so hateful, I wanted to shut her trap with a kiss and never let go.

The night went on with Hobbes and I drunkenly squawking back to the news between bites of pizza, each of us six beers deep. Eventually, Hobbes fell asleep on the couch, so I used my Mind Tap to turn off the news and lovingly took Hobbes's unfinished beer, downed it, then gently carried him to his igloo. Up alone now, it was time to retire to bed. When you're an overseeing voyeur, you watch so much content, the images in your head start losing focus and blur. With my brain bloodshot, I lay under my covers without a hope to get a wink of sleep. The colors I conjured onto the ceiling splattered and danced into symbols and movies. I saw Alexandra and I dancing and realized how damaged my dream glands were. In a perfect world, I would watch less and dream more. I needed a clear, consuming experience and image to nullify my depression. My Mind Tap splashed a film onto my ceiling. There they were, a couple of lovers in breathtaking detail, a sweeping scene, a waltz through a meadow, flowers at their feet, doves fluttering above our heads. I watched, a little teary eyed, wondering what the chances were Alexandra dreamed of me.

Even though I spent the entire night channel surfing, I didn't feel one bit tired by the time I had to get ready for work. Something about the texture of the images projected were so tranquilizing, I might as well have been closing my eyes.

I got dressed in my usual gray button-down shirt. Short sleeves so my supervisors could ogle my tattoos. Then navy blue slacks and a black leather belt with a silver ampersand buckle. I didn't groom my hair; it's best looking crazed in all its gray, frenzied curls. My hair is merely a trap for whatever fingers dare linger through. I grabbed my briefcase, and before heading out the door, I caught a glimpse of myself in the mirror. I looked good. Good enough to insert myself into Alexandra's simulation today. Something I've done many times before, posing as different characters. I texted TK to code me in, and when he asked me how, I told him to surprise me. I kissed Hobbes on his cold, sleepy head and left.

"Tzeep," Hobbes grumbled goodbye and good riddance.

Opening the door to my apartment, I stepped into the apartment's capsule to take me to the ground floor. The news projected against the glass during my quick ride down. Anarchists were preparing to attack. I shook my head as the capsule reached the bottom. Within seconds, a car arrived at the capsule doors. I held my breath as I passed between the capsule and the car because I don't like wearing masks while I'm out. I prefer my drives to be silent too because Alexandra's day would be filled with plenty of music. Silence or faint white noise is the best sound-track for the world of 2066. The sky was blue, the city was green and the air was by no means clean. On a microscopic level, there was an endless war being waged. Invisible killers on suicide missions looked for bodies to detonate inside. The wrong breath in the wrong place could kill you. Alexandra, of course, knew noth-ing of this misery.

I arrived at my office's door, stepped out of the car, held my breath, and had my supervisors unlock the entrance for me step in. The federal building was a towering behemoth of metal and glass. Whatever architectural category modern aesthetics fall under; it was a negligible one. Not worth any sort of analysis or dog-ear in the books of art history. This building, like every new building, wasn't meant to be appreciated. In many ways, observing Alexandra's life was a vacation from this hell hole.

I entered my office and saw Sylvia on the other side of the glass. She pulled away from her screen, nodded at me, and grabbed her things before leaving. Noth-ing interesting must've happened in Alexandra's world that night. Sylvia would've told me if anything out of the ordinary occurred. However, when I sat in front of my screen, I immediately noticed three disturbing phenomena. Alexandra's pencil sharpener was pointing to the right, not the left. Alexandra usually drew in pen, so perhaps she intended to erase whatever she drew. Unless, she didn't use the pencil to draw at all. A pencil makes a great shiv after all, capable of leaving a more permanent scar than any pen. Just this alone was suspect. Second, the window was open two inches higher than she usually had it when she slept. Did she try to escape and carelessly left the window more open when she realized it was impossible? Maybe she was feeling warm, which was strange because we kept it a cool 68 de-grees in her room. Lastly, there was a gray hair in her brush. It could not have been hers. If Alexandra was growing gray without me knowing, then immediate inter-vention was necessary. Aging would surely drive Alexandra deeper into depression. Such a thing could not stand. These were the three glaring issues I reported to my supervisors. I don't know why Sylvia failed to mention any of this. She could be fired for negligence not reporting these potential catastrophes. I reviewed the tape of Sylvia watching Alexandra overnight and noticed at one point she scratched her nose. This was strictly forbidden. Scratching a nose was considered coded language by most master voyeurs. Whoever was watching her could've read that a multitude of ways. I had to snitch on Sylvia and make sure she was let go. Perhaps things would be best if I didn't sleep at all and watched Alexandra all night. Other than what I already noted, the usual pattern of nighttime behavior was there. Nothing special. A few splotches of blood on her pillow. Bite marks on the pit of her hand. Medication taken at double the dose. Only placebos, of course.

She woke up with her usual three long blinks. Every morning, her face had this look of disbelief that she woke up in her body and world one more time. She got up gracefully, too limber for so soon after waking. She then went into her bathroom to brush her teeth, shower, and prepare her face. Her skin was white, but for her to be comfortable in it, she'd have to make herself as pale as possible. Bone white. Alabaster. The essence of goth. Not whiteness but blankness. Frailty. Death. Illness. Vulnerability. Grief. You're not supposed to make yourself look like a corpse, you need to go deeper into death and become a ghost. When the cadaverous foundation she applied made her flesh spectral enough that her lips were the only part of her that looked alive, she stepped out of her bathroom, ready to get dressed.

Her naked body was perfect. Boney in parts like her rib cage, clavicle, and shoulder blades. Fleshy in others like her perfectly round butt. She would choose her outfit by whatever goth subgenre the day felt like. Her wardrobe spanned the entire perimeter of her room as every wall could be pulled back to reveal a closet. She chose nineties goth, meaning a black lace choker with a silver ankh medallion, black leather jeans designed to be worn in underground London clubs after midnight, platform black boots that could catwalk atop tar, and a black sleeveless shirt with white blotches that almost looked like a Rorschach butterfly. This was Nu-Goth. A look for nocturnal flocks of Batcave hacktivists. Half Matrix ala Trinity, half Sandman ala Death. She could do many things with her raven black hair, often teasing it to pretend she was going out to a show. Today she kept it straight, so it ran the length of her back.

She started her day off the way she always does and took a picture of herself to post on Instagram. Her smile was the correct length to indicate she was in a good mood. The likes and supportive comments came pouring in, and we made sure no compliment was ever repeated.

This was the part of the job I loved. I opened up a new window on my screen to send her messages while I watched her. Toggling between different Instagram accounts, I posted comments strategically to motivate her actions. The first comment I wrote was as a boy named Allister Frown. I was an English teenager with a crush. Too fat to ever score a beauty such as Alexandra, she pitied me and patronized my worship with a like, sometimes even a wink. The first thing I wrote was, "Wow, Alexandra … you look like an Egyptian Goddess." I watched her hold her phone close, biting her lip, thinking of what to write. Her fingers started tapping at the screen feverishly. She liked the comment and replied, "Just call me Serket." Serket was a scorpion goddess, invoked by those in need of healing, and to know Alexandra was to know she was a healer. The pain she carried with her was everyone's pain bundled up into an unspeakable mass that occupied her chest and weighed her down so low she could barely stand on her own two feet. Yet, to other people, she showed nothing but kindness. Only able to exude healing vibrations, she used every fiber of discipline in her body so as not to let her pain seep out and find a new host. I went on to message her privately under two different accounts. First as Felix Martinez, her Latino boyfriend studying literature at Columbia University in New York. Felix was always humble enough to credit Alexandra as the real genius between the two of them. This was certainly the case when it came to books. Alexandra could teach a class in creative writing, English, or American and European literature. Her favorite writers were classical. Henry James, Jane Austen, Virginia Wolf. She loved the goths of French poetry as well, Rimbaud, Baudelaire, Comte De Lautreamont. All these influences made her ripe to write herself, which was the only thing that kept her living aside from our tiny, fake romances.

"God, you look too hot today," I messaged her.

"Thanks, but which God?" she joked back.

"What are you up to do today?" I asked.

"I'm about to blog about love. What about you?" She was always writing about love.

"I need to read a book by a Russian author. Any recommendations?"

"Lolita by Vladimir Nabakov."

"Isn't that book about pedophilia?"

"And class dispersity. You'd like it. Nabakov collected butterflies."

There was no creature that disgusted me more than the butterfly. I don't know why she's so obsessed with them. People are so caught up in the beauty of their wings they fail to see how ugly the damn things actually are. I know this because I've seen them under glass in a virtual museum, one of the very few times my parents ever took me anywhere.

"I look forward to your blog post," I wrote before signing off and switching accounts to Jasmine, Alexandra's greatest nemesis.

Alexandra knew the importance of having an impressive set of enemies. Jasmine was republican royalty. She spoke English, Mandarin, Russian, and French. Alexandra's friends had to be exceptionally smart, but her enemies could be nothing short of genius. When I opened our chat log, I saw Alexandra already typing, so I made sure to text her quick and undermine her opening jab.

"good morning, wuv," I wrote.

She stopped typing for a moment and paused, perturbed. She then deleted everything she was planning to send. There was nothing Alexandra hated more than poor grammar, internet acronyms, and neologisms. To her, these things were insults to the English language, and English was the tool that set her free. That's why, even though she was a leftist, she thought the way her comrades misused language was nothing short of criminal.

"Why did you have to go and ruin the rest of my day?"

"I'm jk, bb."

She nearly had a conniption, throwing her phone across the room. This was good. She needed to put her phone down and get to work so I could report what was really on her mind. Writing meant closing her window so no sounds could disturb her. Below her window, Mr. Simmons, her neighbor, was packing up his station wagon to take his family to the lake. Him and his giant poodle, Roy, waved to her. Mr. Simmons' face was programmed to look like mine but bald and fat.

"Morning. You look glowing on this beautiful day."

"*Glowing with ectoplasm*, I hope." Alexandra laughed. "Thanks, Mr. Simmons, you're looking handsome yourself."

"Make sure you say that when the Mrs. is around. She thinks I need to be spending more time at the gym, but today, I'm taking the family out to the lake."

"That sounds wonderful. I hope you all have fun."

"You're welcome to join us."

"Oh, no thanks. I have to stay home and write."

"Suit yourself. Anytime you have writer's block though, the water clears that right up. The view of the bridge over the lake from the bench inspires me every time."

"I'll keep that in mind. Thanks."

She closed the blinds so fast they fell like a guillotine. She then peered through them for one last look out at the billboard, which now featured a personal injury attorney advertisement that read, "If you've been injured on the job, please call 1-800-666-Ovid for Ovid Winger Attorney at Law" underneath my smiling face and slicked-back hair.

Alexandra shook her head and went to her computer to blog. Goths hate lawyers even more than hippies do. Her computer was an old Mac covered in every goth band sticker imaginable. It looked like the inside of a punk club's men's room. She loaded Wordpress and began tickling the magic out her keyboard.

I sometimes wondered if Alexandra would prefer typing over using a Mind Tap. As smart as she was, without a Mind Tap, she didn't have access to knowledge as immediately as the rest of the world. From what I understood, they attempted to install one in her when she was younger, and it didn't pan out too well. Not only did she short circuit the hardware, but she destroyed the network. We decided it was best she stayed fully human. A phone in her pocket would be the closest she came to being a cyborg like us. She put on the Sisters of Mercy album *Floodland* and blogged up a storm.

Noche, Mi Amour

I'm breaking up with my boyfriend today. He doesn't know yet, but he says he reads these posts, so we'll put his word to the test. He's failed either way though. Being cooped up in here all alone, love isn't an act of commitment. Love is an act of amusement. A fog that creeps in just as lightly as it rolls out. I know I won't break his heart. He'll be happy being left with my pictures. That's close enough to the real thing. All my relationships have been so brief and shallow, I wish I knew how it felt to smash a boy's heart into a thousand pieces. I want that just as badly as a love that lasts forever. I am revolted by the frivolity of these affairs. The sort of love I'm forced to bounce between is the kind Bret Easton Ellis might write about. It's a love that could only take place in Los Angeles. A city where another person or place across town is always calling, and you're urged to leave whoever and wherever you are to chase the chance of something better. I would rather have a New York love, that's why I went for Felix in the first place. New York love is a snobbish pastiche of working class, poor people's love. So long as they pretend, that fake love can last a real lifetime. I hate that I think and feel this way. I want to be innocent or naïve enough to believe love can be everything little girls are told it can be. "Prince Charmings" are magical because they're so rare, but these days, all it takes for a Prince Charming to turn into a toad is a single stupid text. I'm not sure if our standards have become impossibly high or despicably low. It's no wonder definitive love stories like Pride and Prejudice or Anna Karenina have been replaced by rotten Judd Apatow films, or worse, Nicholas Sparks. Even Tim Burton forgot how to tell a love story, and when a romantic like that loses his heart, there's no more hope for this darkening world. I want to believe love is an eternal and destined force above nature.

The hottest goth on the internet, and I'm forced into celibacy. I feel as pretentious as Morrissey. I'd ask you to kill me, but I'm already dead. I've been so emotionally deprived; I want the most melodramatic goth lover in the world. I want a boy that listens to The Legendary Pink Dots song "I Watch You in Your Tragic Beauty" crying, thinking of me. He doesn't have to be handsome; he doesn't have to be rich; he doesn't even need to be smart. He just has to put my life above his. A dry, deadpan sense of humor would be nice too. The perfect man for me is Johnny, the protagonist in Mike Leigh's film Naked. I want to spiral into madness with the likes of such a nihilist.

The album of the day is The Sisters of Mercy's Floodland. I've been listening to it as I write, and the album is rearing "This Corrosion." A choir of heavenly voices drowns me in a wash of goth. I feel the spiritual burn of my own lovelessness. The feeling monks spend their lives suppressing. The track soon drops into an all-out dance banger. Riveting sensuality, the clashing of old guitars and new synths makes for a poetry that hits you like death's fist knocking on your sternum. It's a forced kiss that was secretly desired. If this isn't what sex feels like, reconsider sex and put on the Sisters the next time you're in the mood.

After a brief fit of spasmatic dancing, frolicking as Gothically as Aronofsky's *Black Swan*, I suddenly feel better. I'd put on the Cure's *Pornography* if I wanted to write a post that was sad from beginning to end. That's a sad album. A dark and morbid piece. Raw and edgy enough to push you off any tightropes you've been walking. I'm not sure why Ian Curtis chose Iggy Pop's *The Idiot* to be the last album he listened to before he hung himself. I do understand his viewing of Werner Herzog's *Strozyk* though, the story of a bullied immigrant musician. If I were Ian that night and knew my neck was getting snapped, I would've chosen something a little more morose. Maybe Sun Kil Moon … I'm surprised Mark Kozelek is able to live with himself with such a bleak imagination. Actually, I change my mind, if I really wanted to kill myself, I'd listen to John Lennon's "Imagine." Not just because the song is terrible (the only song that's equally shit is Paul McCartney's "Temporary Secretary") but because people still love it in spite of how awful it is.

I don't know why these posts always bounce around from light to dark, happy to sad. My mood swings only come out in my writing. Otherwise, I'm proud to be cold most of the time. I'm definitely not bipolar, no matter what I've been diagnosed with. To be honest, I wouldn't mind a little bit of mania. It would be a beautiful departure from the sluggish pace of quarantine. I will say though, when I write, the highs are shinning, and the lows can be downright terrifying. I swear I'm not actually a suicide case though. You don't need to reach out to me. I'm just trying to rationalize a world that makes no sense. Why would I be put here just to suffer? Does anyone have an answer to that? Sometimes I think I should try my hand at answering it myself by writing a book. Nabokov considered writing novels as his way of solving riddles he made for himself. Then again, no one reads, so it would just be a waste, like anything …

CHAPTER TWO

It was posts like these that made me wonder if she subconsciously knew she was in a simulation. When everything around you is fake, you get a hunch something is off no matter what you're told. How else would she have been able to intuit the love she gets could only exist in Los Angeles? Her and I are in fact in Los Angeles right now.

She mentioned she's apprehensive to write a book given no one reads anymore. This could be corrected by creating a hashtag where her followers each share what they're reading. That would give her the positive feedback necessary to inspire her to write. When the simulation was programmed, they thought she would've liked to be unique. Unique as a writer, as a living library of literature, and uniquely suffering in the world. How would she have reacted if she learned another writer was stuck in their room with the same illness? It would probably only sadden her. No, if she was going to be lonely, it had to be because no one was as smart as her.

If you ask historians, they will say people didn't read in 2020 because nothing worth reading was produced those last two decades since Y2K. People's frame of mind during that time was incapable of producing lasting interpretations of the world. Things have changed though. Reading is so quick and easy with a Mind Tap; a person can absorb someone else's story in the blink of an eye. In fact, today, the only difference between cinema and literature is that literature allows each Mind Tap to produce images for the individual, while cinema feeds the Mind Tap fixed images produced by the director. I would give anything to plug into Alexandra's imagination and read her book. Writers are more transparent in their storytelling than anywhere else. Stories have a way of telling you things the author didn't intend to share.

Alexandra didn't want to love an English student anymore. She wanted a fellow goth now. I would make a few accounts of various goth men to apply for the position. I would have to brush up on my goth knowledge first because Alexandra would sniff out a fake immediately and choose celibacy before a poser.

***

At exactly noon, it was time to initiate another routine moment that was essential to our data collection. A pebble hit Alexandra's window. She knew exactly who it was. She ran from her bed to lift up her window and pull half her body out to see the mailman, Mr. Darcy, delivering letters, postcards, bills, and packages. Mr. Darcy had my face but with a more muscular body and head full of blond, beautiful hair.

"Gorgeous day," he began.

"I know, doesn't it suck?"

"Not when you're a mailman."

"It does when you're a writer."

"Let's hope it rains tomorrow so you can write something juicy; reading your work is usually the best part of my day."

"Aww, you're too kind. Anything special in the mail today?"

Mr. Darcy sifted through our stack.

"Bills, something from the shroud society — "

"That's my Birthday Party shirt."

"It's your birthday soon?"

"No, The Birthday Party, Nick Cave's band."

"I'll check them out, you always have the best music suggestions." Mr. Darcy reached the end of our mail to find a postcard. "You also got a postcard from Russia."

"Russia? Must be from a fan. What's their name?"

"David ... Says it's for his daughter."

Alexandra looked just as shocked as I was. No postcards from her father were ever discussed with the surveillance department. This could result in a range of unpredictable outcomes. God have mercy. A hunch told me Sylvia must've somehow slipped new coding into the simulation. That's what that scratch of the nose had to signal.

"David is my father," Alexandra told Mr. Darcy with tears she could barely keep from running.

"Really? I suppose I should stop wasting your time so you can read it then."

"Please."

Mr. Darcy quickly walked up to the door, slid the mail into the shoot and rushed away, waving at Alexandra as if trying to get out of her hair.

"Mom!" Alexandra screamed.

It took only a minute for Vera Quinn to collect the mail and walk up the stairs of their gothic mansion to her daughter's room. She knocked on the door.

"Yes dear?"

"I need to see the mail."

Vera opened the door. She looked like an older version of her daughter, only with bangs. She was a goth too, but from an older, purer generation. As soon as she opened the door, Chastity hissed at her.

"This package was all that came for you."

Vera threw Alexandra's package from the Shroud Society onto her bed.

"Hopefully this shirt doesn't have any nasty images on it."

"Where's the postcard from Father?"

"How did you know there was a postcard?" Vera asked, making it clear between the time it took for Darcy to deliver the postcard and Vera to retrieve it, Vera must've been commanded not to hand it over to Alexandra.

"Mr. Darcy told me."

"Mr. Darcy has no business looking through our mail. I'll be sure to tell the post office not to send Mr. Darcy here again."

Chastity hissed at Vera again, her feline teeth glinting with snake venom.

"If you don't give me that postcard, I am going to scream."

"We don't even know if it's really from him."

Alexandra screamed at such a blood curdling volume, it could've shattered minds, let alone glass. This scream only made Chastity angrier until she jumped on Vera and started scratching her to shreds. I glanced away from the screen for a second and caught sight of my bottle of water. A whirlpool was spiraling in the liquid. The laws of physics bent to Alexandra's emotions. I glanced back to the screen and saw Vera run down the stairs, screaming as Chastity chased her. With the door to her room left open and completely unattended, Alexandra contemplated escape … at least so she could get her hands on that postcard. It would've been the first time in years she risked her life by leaving, but her father meant everything to her.

Her feet very slowly inched mere millimeters from where her doorway met the hallway. By the time she reached the point of no return, her feet failed to lift off the ground to free her. Just watching her, you could sense a storm raging inside. Then suddenly, veins snapped open on her face and head. Every object in Alexandra's room — her art, her books, her pillows, and stuffed animals — everything was flying around the room in a fast and turbulent orbit.

"Chastity. Come back," Alexandra said calmly, exhausted by all this anxiety and dejection.

Chastity's ears perked up, and for a moment, she took a pause from terrorizing Vera.

"I said come back," Alexandra repeated, ready to turn the world upside-down.

Chastity quickly bolted up the stairs, back to Alexandra's room to hide underneath the bed. Meanwhile, Alexandra was trying not to let her emotions get the best of her. Situations like these discombobulated her entire nervous system. Suddenly, an alarm rang through the office. Employees were scrambling to the bomb shelter beneath the federal building. We had entered a state of emergency. I chose to stay put though, risking my life to keep watching. Whoever decided to have a postcard from her father arrive in the mail should be shot. Sylvia had the clearance, but who did she know on the inside of the coding department? Alexandra's lip trembled as she waited for her mother to come to her senses and stop a meltdown from happening.

"Mom," Alexandra muttered.

Vera stepped up to the last stair to appear before her daughter.

"Please give me the postcard."

I glanced back over to my bottle of water and saw the water was beginning to boil. Vera slowly stepped forward and shakily extended the postcard to her daughter. Alexandra reached for it, but the moment her hand touched the sharp paper, a syringe was stabbed into her shoulder from behind her. A high-powered, fast-acting sedative was shot up into her by Doctor Yorgos Demetrius, the man who led Alexandra's experiment from her genesis. His hair was tall and straight. His robe was white and long. When she fell to the ground, all the floating objects and the entire simulation dropped too, revealing the pure white, two-story cube Alexandra was existing in all along. Outside that pure white cube was a pure white studio space with a few white workers around. The white workers marched through her house to Alexandra's side so they could pick her up and put her in her bed where straps automatically locked her in so she could sleep undisturbed and have her brainwaves mellowed out. With Alexandra sedated, Vera found herself off the job as she sat on the white steps sobbing, trying to collect herself. It was moments like these that confirmed taking this job was a poor life decision.

Doctor Yorgos walked over to her, shaking his head. "I'm sorry. I don't know who programmed this to happen."

"You mother fuckers don't pay me enough to do this. I don't know how much longer I can be part of this sick abuse."

"You earned a bonus today. She'll be out for at least twenty-four hours. Go ahead and take the rest of the day off."

"Thank you." Vera wiped away her tears and flew down the stairs to get the hell out of there as quickly as possible. I looked back at my water, and it was completely flat. Out of nowhere, a hand fell upon my shoulder. I jumped forward and turned around to see three government goons behind me.

"Mr. Ovid, please come with us."

"Don't tell me they think it was me."

"You can ask them yourself what they think."

I let out a deep sigh and followed the three goons out of my office to a capsule, which all four of us shared down to the basement floor. Among the inner circles of government, the basement was known more crudely as the dungeon.

"Aren't you guys afraid I could get you sick?" I asked, seeing as none of us were wearing protection, and we were all hunkered so close.

"No," the goon replied robotically.

I was silent the rest of the capsule ride. When you work a confidential job, anything you say can be interpreted in whatever way they need to use against you. The capsule arrived at the dungeon, and when the doors slid open, the four of us walked down a long steel hallway until we reached a large steel door. The dungeon earned its name with a slew of barbaric and archaic weapons adorning the walls, the blood still crusted over each blade. They opened a door to reveal a darkened room with an angry wooden chair and a lightbulb hanging from the ceiling, laughing every time it swung. They turned the lightbulb on to illuminate the room whereupon I saw a glass wall sitting in front of the chair to separate myself from those that watch watchers like myself. These were my supervisors, I knew them well, Mary Wong and Lisa Charon.

"Sit," Mary commanded me.

The three goons left so my interrogation could begin. My supervisors stepped into the light to reveal they were dressed and styled perfectly. Not a wrinkle in their perfectly starched business attire, not a strand of hair out of place from their pulled-back buns. Lisa was a white redhead. Mary was an Asian blonde. This sort of uniformity, perkiness, iron fist, and steel will were the marks of classic fascist dominators, a look my supervisors foxily calculated.

"Can you explain to us what just happened?" Lisa began.

"From what I observed — "

"We don't care about what you observed. We want what you know," Mary interrupted.

"They're one and the same with simply one detail of difference."

"Which is what?"

"Last night, my afterhours substitute, Sylvia, scratched her nose."

"And?"

"When was the last time you ever saw *me* scratch *my* nose? Or an ear? Or my ass? Never. That's because such a gesture is clearly code."

"Meant for who to see?"

"My guess is someone in programming. Maybe TK."

"Has TK ever coded anything in for you?" Mary took note.

"Only minor additions like my face making cameos in her sim."

They stood there for a second, pretending to take my plea seriously but really not considering the possibility I was telling the truth for even a moment.

"We still think it was you that placed the postcard there," declared Mary, like I hadn't just acquitted myself.

"We don't appreciate your little conspiracy theory either," Lisa said, shaking her head. "Sylvia has worked for us for over a decade. Before the surveillance department, she was closely involved in Alexandra's development."

"All the more reason she would intervene in Alexandra's sim." I shrugged like it was obvious.

"You've gotten too bold. Your ego is blinding you to the purpose of this experiment and the limitations of your job. I don't want to see any more characters or billboards with your face," Mary explained.

"Since I'm sure you've already instructed the programmers to change the coding, so I won't ever appear in her world again, what do you want *me* to do?"

"Shut up. Don't get wise."

"I'm not trying to be wise. I didn't do it. Any time I've requested changes to coding, they've been totally harmless."

"Harmless? You've been grooming the experiment."

The thought that my affection was so obvious totally frazzled my defenses. "Pfft. What? Come on. You don't think … I'm a professional. I have absolutely no feelings for any subject I've ever watched."

"We've seen you in bed. We know how you feel."

I sighed so heavily my breath hung my head down to my lungs' level. I dared not raise my eyes to look at them. Humiliation was their goal and ultimately a necessary lubricant for any subject to tell the truth.

"There are many kinds of love, ladies. I would never do anything to hurt Alexandra, and certainly any kind of romance we could have together would only cause her pain." I found the courage to lift my head after sharing such emotional drivel. "So, look. I'm innocent. I didn't send that postcard."

"We can't prove you did," Lisa concluded.

"We can kill you though, just to cover our asses," Mary chimed in.

My heart seemed to stop. I went cold. I knew what they were capable of. If the government wanted you gone, they didn't care to remove you cleanly. They'd leave traces of you behind just to send a message for the rest of the staff not to be a pain in their ass. I heard stories about a spy whose emails were compromised, so they skinned him alive in a chicken coop and covered him in bird seeds before releasing a troop of hungry hens.

"Don't worry, we're not going to kill you." Mary laughed.

"Thank you," I said after exhaling a breath I forgot I was holding in.

My blood warmed up, kick-starting my heart with a relieving shock.

"We could fire you though," Lisa continued.

This rollercoaster of emotion was too much for my soft temperament to handle. My organs clenched up, clunkily dragging every time they tried to contract and expand. Being in the dungeon felt like you were strapped to some kind of invisible torture rack.

"We're monitoring your heart, you know."

Suddenly, my heartbeat projected against the glass that separated us. It started running faster the moment they showed this to me.

"Don't be nervous."

My heartbeat steadied.

"But we're going to punish you."

I gripped my chest, worried I might just keel over.

"We will be censoring Alexandra's body after this. You can't be trusted seeing her nude."

"She never actually excited me anyway."

"Sure … now get back to work," Mary finished.

"We'd tell you to get out of our sight, but that's impossible." Lisa winked.

"I'll make you very happy with my work from here on. Forgive all my transgressions."

They smiled and nodded. I nodded back and slyly escaped my chair. The steel door opened to the three goons, and as soon as I saw them, my heart rate spiked on the glass. They escorted me all the way back to my screen where Alexandra was sleeping soundly. The workers were still reassembling her room, putting all the books back in place.

Interested to see her reading, I made Alexandra's heartbeat appear onscreen. Although her heart beat once every ten seconds, there was no need to worry about

Alexandra dying. We'd never let any serious harm come to her. I've actually heard she is immortal. A call window popped up on screen. It was TK from coding. I swallowed hard and answered. TK's face was distinctly tortured, with a bulbous nose, cretinous black ponytail, numerous scars, and a cleft lip balanced by mutton chops on either side of his face.

"Dude, what did they do to you?" he asked.

The funny thing about surveillance is that because everyone knows they're being watched, people are always honest. When you act like you have something to hide, they start asking questions. It was in this way, telling lies became a rarely practiced freedom.

"They took me into this tiny little room with my supervisors and asked if I sent that postcard. You told them I didn't, right?"

"Yeah, I told them I'm the only one you request code from. And I didn't code it in."

"You removed my face and censored nude scenes, right?"

"Sorry man."

"It's cool. I told them I thought it was you and Sylvia."

"No problem, asshole. Now they won't suspect us."

"So, who do you think did it?"

"Not the plumber," he said, scratching his nose.

Plumber was coded language, just like scratching your nose. It meant he knew. A bead of sweat formed on my temple and ran down the side of my face, knowing they could easily catch onto us. One little mistake and we could end up working in a Martian chain-gang.

"Have they started their investigation?" I asked.

"They confiscated a bunch of old drives to review. I think they're going to hire a new supervisor for my department too."

"That sucks."

"Yeah. Hey, I got a question for you — who watches out for the watchers?"

"We have a union."

I got back to my apartment late. There was a whole new process to clock out of work after the day's debacle. Everything from a vision exam to a urine sample was required. When I opened my door, I was met with total silence. This was strange. Hobbes had been freezing all day and would've been running for my leg like he always does. I went over to his igloo and bent down to look inside. It was empty.

"Hobbes?" I exclaimed, trying to summon him.

Still, there was silence. I began fearing the worst. I should've known my punishment was more severe than a few new restrictions at work.

My Mind Tap commanded my projector to display surveillance footage of my apartment against the wall. Hobbes was lying atop his igloo, staying cool. Suddenly, his eyes snapped open, and he turned to the door. Someone must have knocked. He waddled over to answer it, and a masked intruder threw a sack over him and kidnapped the little guy. The intruder then threw the sack over their shoulder and ran down the hallway. The damn fool, Hobbes knew never to answer the door unless I was home.

I wanted to cry and shake my fist at the heavens, swearing revenge against the penguin snatcher, but instead, I suppressed my anger in case they were watching because unhinged displays of anger could get your name written down on a list. All I could do was sit down and watch the news alone because the only anger acceptable was disdain for the anarchist resistance, now protesting for the thousandth day in a row. They wanted an end to mass surveillance. Fools — such a thing was impossible. Who do they think they are, trying to dismantle our whole way of life? One threw a smoke bomb, another shot rounds at the cyber cops. It was a complete shit show. Then I saw something I must've hallucinated because there were three anarchists, a lady, a man, and a midget that were fighting. The man and woman pulled down their masks for a second, and though they had face paint on, they looked exactly like Sylvia and TK. After putting their masks back on, they started shooting automatic rounds. I figured I must be seeing things, after all, there were tears in my eyes.

When I got back to work, Alexandra was already awake, and Sylvia was long gone. There was a harmony in her simulation, like nothing ever happened. I put two screens side by side to review whatever I missed before she woke up. Her straps unlocked and retreated back into her bed the moment she started to stir. When she opened her eyes, she groaned as if her tantrum drained her body of life. That day, she decided to do her makeup in Batcave goth style, using eyeliner to draw the Egyptian Eye of Horus around her right eye. She teased her hair too, taking on a banshee quality. Her fashion followed in that eighties vein with black leather, fishnets, and chains around her waist. She went to close the window, and Mr. Simmons wasn't there to greet her, having been deleted for carrying my face. Instead, a new family was moving in next door. The billboard at the edge of the city featured a new advertisement for a plumber, with Sylvia holding a plunger slung over her shoulder. This was some kind of terrible tease. The plumber's number was 323-we-drain. I knew this was a message from TK. I memorized the number so I could call him later tonight.

Alexandra put on Bauhaus's *In the Flat Field*. She was feeling especially dubious, as if her next blog post would do someone some kind of harm.

Sounding the Seventh Trumpet

I got so mad the other day I could've killed someone. I always let my temper get the best of me; I can't help it. In some ways, it's a sign of arrested development. Being confined to this stupid room, I inevitably outgrew it a long time ago, but because there's no place else for me to stay, I am forced to stagnate here and never become the beautiful butterfly I am meant to be. It's like I'm trapped in my cocoon. It's better I stop wishing I was a butterfly altogether and just assume the life of a spider. So, sometimes I lash out, and when I do, the only way I can come back to my senses is sleep. I'll sleep for days sometimes, just for a shred of peace. I love to sleep on the off chance I'll be lucky enough to give up control to a dream.

Last night, I dreamed I drove a hearse, complete with a coffin in the trunk. I drove that hearse down the coast, up Big Sur, to view the most vibrant scenes of earth and sea. As soon as I remembered no one ever taught me how to drive, I took a sharp turn off the side of a cliff. Free falling to my demise, I lit a cigarette and let the ground come to me. Instead of forcing myself to wake up and avoid death, I embraced the end for all it was worth just to see if I'd wake up or not.

Waking up sucks without the lovely goth boy of my dreams next to me. I want one that doesn't need to put on any makeup. I want their normal state of being to be pale and sickly. A hemophiliac would make a good boyfriend. I want them to wear black like it is their second skin, not a statement. An accent wouldn't hurt

either. An English one preferably. You have to be an Anglophile to be goth. Dreary
England is where it all happened. Fog, rain, European decadence, and industrial
hopelessness are necessary ingredients to goth music. I put on Bauhaus's first record, *In the Flat Field*. I wouldn't mind dating the naked Peter Murphy sounding
a horn on the album's cover. The first song on the record is the ultimate represen-
tation of goth aesthetics. "Dark Entries," with its moody, hazy guitars and haunting vocal, you get the impression you're in some dungeon cell that hasn't seen
sunlight since its gates were rusted shut. I like to imagine my room turning into
such a dungeon. Shadows spilling out of every opening and coating the walls, ceiling, and floor in black. I suspend myself upside down like a vegan fruit bat whenever I listen to this record. The album's next track, "Double Dare" has to play at
my wedding. It's disorienting, sensual, sexual, and downright savage in moments.
I play it so loud and late it has the whole neighborhood waking up to call the
police, but even they're too freaked out to knock on the door that stands between
them and this forbidden music. It's on this track where we see goth take on its
most animalistic character. Goths appear rather cultured in public, but in the darkness of privacy, once we've shed those frilly clothes, we take on a violent and sexual
sort of poetry. You will see scratches on our naked bodies. The crashing of the
drums on this track is peak angry Alexandra. Only now, I channel that anger into
wild dancing. I'm trying to disturb my mother, make sure she knows to stay clear
of me. Just in case Bauhaus isn't frightening enough, I'll put on Suicide's *Frankie
Teardrop* next and make sure she knows I mean trouble.

CHAPTER THREE

Noon came and went without Mr. Darcy's pebble ever hitting Alexandra' window. She looked through the blinds to see the new mail woman with Sylvia's face delivering her a thin stack of bills. She found herself so outstandingly bored, crying seemed to be the only way to amuse her. When she wouldn't cry, she would stare at the ceiling, walls, or floor. Her vision would hone in on the tiny civilizations living in her carpet, the mites eating her dead hair and skin, begging for a drop of blood to fall so they could leech off something more substantial. They'd have to settle for tears. Feeling sorry for these tiny companions, she got up off her bed and reached under her bed. Her razors were gone though, taken by a thief in the night. She began to scramble, huffing and puffing when she realized there would be no relief. No decompression. No bloodletting. Not knowing where her utensils went or who took them, she slammed her fist against her bed. A tremor ran through my glass of water. I gulped hard, anticipating another shit storm. She took her disappointment with stride though, simply lying back down and putting on a record. Dead Can Dance's *Aion*. Their music was inspired by ancient sounds from across the world. I could see her soul embarking on a spiritual journey as her body laid totally still. During "Song of the Sybil," Lisa Gerard's voice soared with such sacred pain that Alexandra could feel every stinging octave in her blood. It hurt so bad, she needed it out. She closed her eyes and clenched her teeth, visualizing in her mind a knife and psychically forming an invisible one out of thin air. With it, she cut tiny slits up and down her arms. Each slit splattered blood all over her body and bedding. Once that first gush gave her the orgasmic release of trading emotional pain in for physical, she opened her eyes to let out her tears and with surgical precision, psychically stitched every one of her cuts back up like nothing happened. Everything was covered in fresh blood, but nothing was bleeding.

It always makes me queasy to watch her do this to herself. I brought my trash bin up to my mouth and spit up my lunch. The rest of the day, she stared up at the ceiling like it was a blank page, barely moving until a knock came at her door.

"Princess," Vera spoke through the door.

"Yes, Mom?"

"I brought you dinner. Can I come inside?"

"No. Just leave it on the floor, and I'll get it."

"Okay. No problem. I love you."

Alexandra thought for a second then replied, "I love you too, Mom."

It must've been another hour before she got up to take her dinner. She had a vegan casserole and beet salad. She found beets particularly goth, stabbing one with her fork and bringing it to Chastity's mouth. Chastity refused the beet and jumped off her bed to prowl over to the window.

"What's wrong? Aren't you hungry?"

Chastity hissed at the window, and Alexandra got up to see what she was so bothered by. She was taken aback because at the edge of the sill was a white butterfly, sitting there with its wings flapping slowly and poetically. An expression fell over Alexandra's face I had never seen before. It was awe. This was the first butterfly she'd ever seen in person. This butterfly couldn't have been part of the recent bug fixes. I was sure this was going to be blamed on me too. Butterflies were symbols of many things, none of which were appropriate for Alexandra to be exposed to. In prisons, a butterfly tattoo is reserved for those that know the way out. White butterflies, specifically, symbolize that the dead are watching over you. Worst of all, in certain underground circles, butterflies mark victims of mind control. They are symbols of the other side, and God forbid Alexandra ever learned any other sides existed. I looked more closely at the butterfly and noticed something especially strange. The creature didn't conform to the rest of the simulation. With every bat of its wings, the fake layer of simulation all around it would distort. This could mean that somehow, an actual butterfly found its way into the experiment. Everyone assigned to this case had nightmares something like this could happen someday. Luckily for us, Alexandra didn't seem to understand the gravity of what she was witnessing. She just smiled and cried a bit. Chastity jumped at the butterfly and swiped at it, but the butterfly flew off its perch into the fraudulent sky. Alexandra bid it farewell until her door flew open. She turned around and saw Doctor Yorgos standing there with his syringe. Moments that were not meant to be must be erased. This mantra marked every appearance Yorgos would ever make in her sim. Alexandra subconsciously recognized his face and the syringe but had no idea who he was.

"Who are you? What do you want?"

The doctor stepped forward and stabbed her with the sedative before her mind could tear him to bits. Once she fell to the ground, unconscious, he let out a long sigh of relief that he made it out alive. For whatever reason, the powers that be never requested my presence to interrogate me about this issue. They must've known I had no involvement with the butterfly. This made me suspicious though; a pattern of behavior was broken. Whoever brought that butterfly into laboratory seven and compromised the experiment must've had the highest security credentials. The people with such credentials were mostly scientists, with a few exceptions, one of them being Vera. The first thing I did when I got home was sift through the federal building's directory and meticulously went through every security camera to follow Vera's tracks after she finished her shift. She took a capsule to the garage where transport was waiting for her. I noted the car's license plate and was able to wrangle a list of all the places it had been that day. After its trip to the federal building, it took a long ride out of downtown to an address on Cherry Street. I found the home on a map, and it was a near replica of Alexandra's simulation. A gothic house on a gothic hill. I decided I'd call the house.

"Hello, Vera?" I began.

"Yes. Is this the plumber?" she replied.

I thought for a second and realized she must've meant the same plumber on Alexandra's billboard. I decided to play along.

"Yes," I dropped my voice a lower register. "I did as you requested. The butterfly is inside."

"Good."

"Is there something else you need from me?"

"If anything comes up, I'll call again."

I hung up the phone and called the plumber's number straight away.

"If it's clogged, we'll drain it." It was TK's voice on the other line.

"Why did you tell Vera to bring Alexandra a butterfly?"

"The answers to all your questions are in the igloo."

Just like that, he hung up. My eyes floated over to the igloo where Hobbes once rested his blessed head. I walked over to it and bent down to reach inside. I felt around and found a thick pile of papers bound together by brass braids. It was a manuscript, and on the front was written "Goth Girl by Alexandra Quinn."

Goth Girl

When I was really little, I wasn't allowed to have hair. They shaved my head, my arm pits, my eyebrows, everything. I looked like a fetus, but never felt embarrassed about it. It's not like I was sent to school looking this freakish. All my friends were scientists, and they accepted me. My best friend, Doctor Yorgos Demetrius would give me different candies every day, and when I cried, he'd cheer me up with a story about animals. I quickly came to love bats under his tutelage.

I never knew my parents. I was assigned a mother that would take care of me and call me her daughter, but in reality, I was a test tube baby. I was a specimen, manufactured to be a weapon, but after I failed certain tests, they deemed me in-eligible for combat. I would suffer enduring these tests, but the advances made from the data collected put an end to the suffering of others. The first tests I un-derwent were rather harmless. They'd stick me in a white room with three colored toys. A red stuffed dog, a yellow bird, and a blue bat. They drew a circle on the floor around me and each of the animals at the other end of the room. I would plead and beg to hold the blue bat, but any time I tried to leave the circle, I would start feeling ill. First a burning in my stomach, then that fire would travel up to my lungs and head until it overwhelmed me. If I returned my body to the circle, these symptoms would subside almost immediately. Having not been taught to speak yet, I could only moan to ask them to let me have the cute blue bat. They always refused my begging until one day, I held my hand out to the bat, and with every ounce of mental and emotional fortitude in my small being, I communed with the world to bring the bat to me. Suddenly, like magic, the bat trembled on the ground just as my hand trembled reaching for it. Veins started growing up and down my outstretched arm, body, face, and bald head. When the bat finally sprang off the ground and flew through the air, directly into me, I held it so tightly and close to my chest that no scientist was strong enough to pry it from my grasp. I named him Vamp.

Eventually, they put me through courses to develop this skill and I learned it had a name: Telekinesis. I was telekinetic, but even more than that, I was psychic. I didn't fully grasp the meaning of these words, but I accepted them as part of my identity. At this stage of my development, that's all I had. After a week, I could pull and push the other stuffed animals to and away from me. After two weeks, my mind was able to do tricks with the animals, making them dance. After a month, I could puppeteer them to interact and move like humans might. They brought male and female volunteers into my room and sat them around a table. They then had me try to mimic the conversation between them with the red dog and yellow bird. I made the two conversations mirror images of each other, manipulating every wave of the hand or wag of the foot to be exactly the same. There were certain moments I couldn't recreate though, tiny nuances of the face, like a glint in the eye. These subtle expressions between the boy and girl seemed deeply mysterious. I was curious what they meant and where the feelings that inspired them came from. Was I capable of such human expressions, or was I another stuffed animal? When the couple gently kissed, I paused. The discipline it took for me to control things with my mind was broken for the first time. Tears formed in my eyes. I felt like such a failure for crying over something so trivial, I psychically sent those tears flying to opposite corners of the room. I passed the test with a grade of only eighty five percent for mucking up the end. From this grade, they concluded I was not the perfect weapon I was born to be, even after all the manipulation and deprivation, I still somehow had enough heart to recognize humanity when I saw it. I somehow made a promise to myself, not knowing what a promise even was. I promised I would find a love who would kiss me forever. I didn't know the concepts of promise, love, or forever. I only knew the concept of kiss. Still, I felt this truth in my core. They could've disposed of me after determining I was ineffective for their purpose, but for some reason, they must've thought I was still worth studying.

After completing beginner's telekinesis, I graduated into intermediate and advanced evaluations, culminating in learning to navigate a pencil with my mind to draw. My drawings became incredibly realistic depictions of fantastic hells that intrigued and perplexed my doctors. They knew something grand must be going on inside me, so finally, they decided I should learn to write. First, I'd have to learn a language so I could speak and read. Having never been exposed to television, as soon as I picked up English, it became my only form of entertainment and amusement. The way I could interchange words to make sentences felt, to me, like playing with toys. I'd play all day with my teacher, a beautiful English woman named Sylvia. Among the scientists, she was called my linguistics instructor, but she used to call herself my nanny. After learning how to speak using an elaborate card matching game, I acquired a British accent just like hers. It's too bad it disappeared when I no longer required her teaching — now I just have a crude, strange hybrid Anglo-American sounding voice. Not that it mattered considering how quietly and shyly I usually project it. Sylvia taught me words were always inside of me. Words like "sadness" or the synonym I prefer, "sorrow," for its rhythm. Sylvia showed me the books that identified all my pains and heartaches. The great novels of humanity, books from all around the world, spanning centuries. They taught me everything I needed to know about love and hate. After all the tests, abuse, and memory wipes, I never lost the words Sylvia taught me. Once she was relieved of her duties as my nanny and they stuck her in some boring job in surveillance, that's when she began planning my escape. The first step required to set me free was to remind me how much we used to love each other. It wasn't until she made herself known to me, hiding clues in my simulation, that I remembered her face again. When she convinced me to write the story of my life by manipulating a pencil to write on my ceiling, all my lost memories flooded back to me in a great emotional upswell.

The men that created my jail cell think setting me free could kill millions of people, as if one of my mood swings could cause a tantrum that psychically devastates everything around me. I understand their concern, but I swear on my life, if I was in love, I would never hurt a fly. Everyone surveilling me, except Sylvia, never realized I was writing on my ceiling. I would psychically remove all the graphite before morning when Sylvia's shift was over. By then, the one camera that was pointed at the ceiling would take a picture of my finished page to be transcribed into my book.

Sylvia told me if I wrote a memoir, she could get it out to the world and cause an uproar demanding my freedom. So, I wrote *Goth Girl*. It was a story the world never heard before. Stories like mine are always suppressed because they threaten the powerful with mass revolution.

Mine was the story of a failed weapon. Born to kill without feeling, I developed a heart that thwarted all their dehumanizing efforts until one day they realized I had the potential to be something greater than even they intended. When I turned thirteen, I had effectively learned every skill I needed for my own existence, mastering my psychic abilities. So, one day, they brought in a real live monkey to test by my side. This monkey had a prototype for the Mind Tap installed in its brain. The Mind Tap would read neurological signals then communicate them to objects using a wireless connection. They had me use my abilities and then asked the monkey to mimic me. When it wanted to drink a bottle of soda that was across the room, the monkey held out its hand like I did, and the soda would come to it. The Mind Tap was inspired by my abilities; I was the muse for a new way man could use technology. The operating system the entire world would connect with was merely a tribute to my powers. Now, any human can do what I do, so long as they have a Mind Tap. However, to avoid humans causing the havoc I've been known to create, those with Mind Taps are monitored day and night, having their emotions and thoughts watched, if not completely controlled. What the Mind Tap could do that not even I was capable of, was gain access to the internet's trove of knowledge. After numerous tests beside the monkey, Doctor Yorgos came into the lab to talk to me.

"Alexandra, would you like to have every book ever written in the library of your mind?"

"You mean I wouldn't have to wait for you to bring me books anymore?"

"Exactly."

"I would love that."

"Okay. This won't hurt a bit."

Doctor Yorgos pulled out a syringe, bigger than the one he usually administered my sedative with and injected me with a clear liquid that put me to sleep for an entire day.

During my slumber, I had the strangest dream. I was alone on the moon. It seemed like familiar terrain. I knew how to walk around on its surface, my bare feet felt at home with lunar dust between my toes. Even though it was only a dream, I spent only a few hours of sleep in this person's body, I somehow knew my own history. I was born on the moon. I never saw any other people, and I never knew love. As much as I liked the warmth of bathing in the sun's rays and watching the Earth, the frozen permanent night of the moon's dark side is where

I found peace. I would sleep there, letting the darkness be my blanket from all the scary things that could happen to someone out in the light. Eventually, as I strolled between the craters, I finally saw another person. They were wearing an astronaut's uniform. I walked over to them and looked inside their glass helmet. The astronaut was a man with one eye that appeared blue and the other black.

"How I missed you, moon child," the astronaut said.

"How long have I been gone?" I asked.

"Thousands of years. The Earth is no longer the same."

"I don't ever want to go back," I told him.

"But you must," he replied.

"No!" I shouted and pushed him.

The force of this push lifted his feet off the ground and sent him spiraling off the moon toward the Earth. He never lost momentum, the man that fell to Earth.

I woke up with the Mind Tap installed in my brain. I overheard the scientists say Master was some sort of God now. I wasn't sure what to think about that, but I didn't like it. Besides acquiring all the world's knowledge, the Mind Tap gave me the ability to read the hearts of anyone else with the same tech. So now I could look into this monkey's heart. When I saw the tragedies of his life and the amount of experimentation he was subjected to, it infuriated me so much I wanted to destroy everything in sight. I blew out the Mind Tap in the monkey's brain, wanting to put an end to its suffering, but having never developed the precision required to control my unleashed psychosis, I ended up blowing his whole brain out. All the windows in the laboratory shattered. The very network the Mind Tap used to connect to everything was completely destroyed. There were monkey brains, blood, and glass everywhere. The air fizzled with damaged waves. They sent numerous scientists in to sedate me, and I killed them one by one, blowing each of their heads off until Doctor Yorgos arrived, and I fought the impulse to kill him with every ounce of my being so he could put me to sleep. When I woke up, I had no Mind Tap or memory of my life before that day.

At the age of thirteen, with my memory wiped, the trajectory of these experiments took a dark turn. They decided to test various forms of duress on me to see how my abilities would cope. I would get cut with a knife only for them to watch how I would seal my own flesh back up. During one test, a doctor shot me directly in the chest. The pain was excruciating for the moments it took to expunge the bullet and refill the hole with fresh material. Violence wasn't the only way they would torment me though. They found ways to make pleasure as revolting as pain, beauty as abhorrent as ugliness. For example, they would remove all stimulation but a rose, bird, or a picture of the beach. Whenever I started to enjoy that beautiful thing, they would induce sickness in me until I lost all fondness for it. They tried to do the same with music, but it never worked. Whenever they tried to develop my aversion to music, I would escape deeper into it until I felt no pain, even if my nervous system careened into paralysis. They performed tests I hesitate to write. Their pursuit to collect data on my sexuality broke me into the person you know today. This was when they learned there was a light inside me they could not kill. I never forgot, I just buried it deep.

One experiment involved filling the air with a virus to see how my abilities would respond to transmission or infection. My mind was hypersensitive to harm or change, identifying the virus immediately. Within moments, my mind displaced the viral particles in the air away from me, and my body changed its own molecular structure to stop the virus from seeding.

It's a miracle I haven't lost hope after all this. Not hope for me but hope for humanity. I know someday I'll escape, it's what gets me through my worst nights. Someday, my goth in shining armor will rescue me from this hell. He will be so tender and aware of the pain people experience, he'll be able to point a suffering soul out in a crowd and offer his love without needing to be asked. Even though I'm so broken inside, he'll accept that mending my heart back together is just part of loving me. I don't know who this goth is, but I have a feeling, deep down in my heart, they know me.

CHAPTER FOUR

Holding in my hands the revelation that Alexandra was fully aware of our experiments, I couldn't say I was surprised. So much overt and ego-driven manipulation was done to her, she had to notice the cracks in the code at some point. Anyone would. It's amazing how she never once lashed out against us or the world. She didn't have a vengeful bone in her body. In reality, she was practicing extraordinary discipline, never having killed Doctor Yorgos, even though she had the ability to at the snap of her fingers. Now that I know all this, all I could do was sit back, relax, and wait for someone to take me away to be interrogated. Having assimilated the book's contents into my Mind Tap, everyone with access to it was now also aware of what really made Alexandra tick.

A knock came at the door. I was surprised they came for me so quickly. Before I got up from my sofa, I decided I would play a game with myself and guess who was going to be behind that door. Maybe Lisa and Mary sent their three goons to do their dirty work again. This information was so sensitive though, Lisa and Mary couldn't trust me being escorted without them being present. I strolled over to my door and looked into the peephole. I was wrong. The same mask that donned the penguin snatcher was on the person waiting behind my door.

"You mother fucker," I growled.

I quickly unlocked the door and pulled it open.

"Who the hell do you think you are, stealing my best friend?" I began.

The penguin snatcher glanced down at my feet, forcing my eyes down with theirs. Below was Hobbes, pointing a gun up at me. I was shocked.

"Little buddy?"

He fired a tranquilizer dart directly into my forehead. It hurt like a reverberating hell.

"What was that for?"

I grabbed the dart and pulled it out of my skin. It took a bit of effort to pluck it out, and once I did, the hole started leaking blood.

"Was that supposed to knock me out?" I drowsily slurred.

The penguin snatcher rolled their eyes, mocking me. Furious but drowsy, I tried to swing at them but found myself tripping over air. I fell onto the ground, bouncing my jaw on the floor, blacking me out.

***

When I woke up, the first thing I saw was a giant oil portrait of Leo Tolstoy, the Russian author. The first being to greet me was Hobbes, who scurried over to warm up next to me. His glossy eyes looked into mine, and I could tell this was his only way of apologizing.

"It's okay. I forgive you."

To the right was a doorway from which TK emerged. Then to the left, was another doorway that Sylvia entered the room from.

"You two?" I realized my conspiracy theory just materialized before my eyes. "You mean I was right?"

"There's a fucking reason they pay you so much, asshole." TK shook his head.

"I'm the asshole? You guys stole my penguin."

"He's on our side now."

"Sides? There are sides?"

"We're anarchists. Notice the Tolstoy." Sylvia pointed up at it.

I turned to Hobbes in disbelief. "All the times we spent drinking beers and making fun of them, now you've joined their cult?"

Hobbes just shrugged. I then turned to Sylvia.

"And you, how dare you undermine everything we've been hired to do?"

"How dare I? You're the one who claims to love the girl, yet all you do is help them destroy her. Us four are the only ones in the whole world that give a shit about her."

"Four?" I asked.

A teenager stepped out from the shadows in front of Sylvia and nodded at me. Just like Alexandra, or any anarchist or goth, he wore all black, only he wore it differently than the rest of our company. His use of black was not a sign of depression but a sign of cool. I believe his glasses were what were known as Ray-Bans.

"Who's the shrimp?"

"My son," proclaimed Sylvia.

"What's he got to do with all this?"

"He hacked Alexandra's simulation," answered TK. "You can blame this kid for the postcard."

"Is that all? Why did you order Vera to bring the girl a butterfly?"

"I've called my son my butterfly. Seeing as he's always on my mind, which is what a white butterfly signifies. Vera hid it in the lab so it could make its way through the simulation and let Alexandra know she's on our minds," Sylvia explained.

"Is Vera an anarchist too?"

"No. She's only trying to help the poor girl. She doesn't exactly subscribe to our beliefs."

"Charlie is a master hacker. His skills even surpass mine." TK smiled.

"Ovid, I hacked your Mind Tap to control any information shared with your bosses. That's why we've thrown them for a loop all this time," Charlie explained.

"You what?" I couldn't believe it.

"If they saw all your memories and thoughts, you wouldn't have made it this far." Charlie smiled as if I should be thankful.

"Holy shit. I'm a dead man." I hung my head.

"We couldn't have done it without my butterfly." Sylvia beamed, resting her hands proudly on her son's shoulders.

"And we can't do it without you either, Ovid." TK glared at me with eyes full of agenda.

"Do what?"

"Rescue Alexandra," Sylvia added.

"Why would you want to do that?"

"Her mind inspired the technology that put the world in chains. Only she can set it free again," Charlie chimed in.

"The human mind is not meant to link itself to anything but nature. With the Mind Tap installed in their brains, humanity's potential reaches only as far as the technology's limit, whereas once it could reach beyond the stars. We miss our intuition. We miss our imagination. We miss our souls. We want them back, and we want the Mind Tap gone forever," TK explained.

"Set free and left to her own devices, Alexandra has the power to kill us all," I rebutted.

"Better than living with the government's boot on our neck," Charlie surmised.

"You're only a kid, what the hell do you know about oppression?"

"Liberation is their deal," Charlie said, gesturing at the adults. "I'm not doing this for any other reason than my fondness for Alexandra."

"Oh, so you're in love with her too? Well, that's just great. Join the club, kid."

"It's a bit too premature for me to love her, wouldn't you say? No. I'd like the chance to take her out on a date is all, treat her like a human being."

"She'll never be like us. If you hacked the simulation, you would know that."

"I don't want her to be like us or even me. Why do you think I introduced her to goth music? The first time she ever heard the Cure was my hacktivism at work."

There was a long silence as I absorbed everything these bastards were telling me. I could sympathize with their cause and even find Charlie's hope to save her endearing, but most of all, the burning hatred I felt against them for stealing Hobbes outweighed any interest I had in making peace.

"You're going to be sorry you were ever so brazen to abduct my penguin. You may have hacked my Mind Tap, but you can't stop me from telling my bosses everything that happened here."

"We didn't just hack your Mind Tap. While you were sleeping, we disabled it."

"You're shitting me."

"Go ahead — look up the altitude in Madrid."

I closed my eyes and tried to think, scouring every inch of my mind for the answer only to realize my mind was reduced to a small and empty room, where every door that was once open wide was now locked shut. I was disabled, in a literal sense. The stupefying nature of technological dependency has left me completely devoid of any knowledge of my own. I could barely tell you who I was at that moment.

"How did you do that?"

TK raised a rather draconian looking instrument, the tip of its sharp hooked drill was covered in blood, most likely mine.

"You stuck that thing in me?"

"To turn it back on, all I have to do is shove it back in and twist a few times."

"But you won't want it turned back on," Sylvia added.

"Yes, I would. Do you know how this feels?"

"I do, I never had one installed at all," said Charlie.

"How have you been able to exist?"

"Anarchists live below the surface and above the law."

"There's no way I would let my son experience this hell," Sylvia stiffly stated.

"Don't worry. Not only will you learn to love this new phase of your life, but you'll finally be able to pursue your destiny."

"Like you know what my destiny is?"

"To help us set her free. That is the goal of the anarchist movement. To free Alexandra so she can disable every Mind Tap in every human in one fell swoop of her psychic scythe."

"No thanks. I'd sooner die than disobey my orders."

"Then we'll simply change those orders. No big deal. You've barely had enough time to start thinking for yourself; in a few days, you'll come around."

"Don't count on it. Am I free to go now?"

"There's the door."

TK pointed behind me, and I turned around to find an open capsule, ready to take me away from these people as quickly possible. I turned back to my penguin.

"Hobbes, let's go."

Hobbes stayed put, crossing his wings over his chest, breaking my heart right on the spot.

"This betrayal is unforgivable."

Hobbes turned his cheek and waddled out of the room before I wallowed into the capsule.

"One last thing before you go … The three of us have a dark wave band called Das Leid. If you like what Alexandra plays, definitely check us out," Charlie said.

"No thanks."

"We uploaded the songs to your Mind Tap. That's the only thing you can still use it for."

"Fuck off," I said before leaving.

Sylvia used her Mind Tap to order the capsule up, and I was shot back to the surface world. The first thought that hit me as I saw the busy streets filled with air-tight cars zipping down the derelict streets was —

"Fuck."

This must be how a blind man feels trying to navigate through the world. The sad thing was that, given the sorry state of the world, blindness and deafness are probably prerequisites to happiness. I stepped out of the capsule, lifting my shirt to use as a mask and flagging myself as a nut, probably an anarchist too, to any cyber cops I'd be unfortunate enough to encounter. I looked back at the building I emerged from; it was a warehouse with all its windows broken out. I started walking down the streets with no idea where exactly I was, staying or going. There was no indication of what street I was on or turning onto. The world had been repurposed for machines a long time ago, and I was merely a man. I knew the longer I stayed out in this hell, the more chances I'd have to choke on the air around me. Finally, I recognized the logo of Zeitgeist pizza. Delivery from Zeitgeist took five minutes after the pizza had been finished, meaning I was five minutes away from my apartment. I wasn't sure which direction my apartment was from Zeitgeist, but something told me to turn right down the next street. As soon as I told myself to run right, I asked myself why. What evidence was there that my home was to the right? What was telling me to go that way? Where such an answer derived from was a complete mystery. I can't remember the last time I came to such a baseless conclusion, not through thinking but feeling. I knew to turn right in my chest, not my head. This is what they'd call intuition. Before today, I lived a life of enough luxury and privilege that there was no use for such a tool. The Mind Tap is more trustworthy than the human heart or spirit, but this feeling was better than nothing, so I ran right. Eventually, I slipped into a giant puddle and hit my face against the street. With my face still masked by my now blood-soaked shirt, I pulled it down to reveal what was probably a broken nose. I looked up, and through my tears, the first time I cried from pain in a long time, I saw my apartment. There it was, so conveniently placed for me to return home and affirm I still felt traces of neural connectivity whether or not I was plugged into the system. I had my Mind Tap installed moments after I was born, meaning I was most free in utero.

When I reached my apartment's capsule, I realized I had no way to instruct it to take me home. I walked along the side of the building, hoping there were stairs, until eventually I found the door. I took those stairs, and by the time I reached the top, I was sweating, crying, and bleeding, broken and disabled but somehow feeling accomplished, even happy. When I finally got back to my home, I went to the bathroom and washed up. No longer a bloody mess, I went back to the living room and fell upon the couch. I realized I couldn't summon the news, so the only thing left to amuse me was Alexandra's book. I felt it draw me in, like this was the most important information I could absorb. This book was the news — it was not only the key to breaking her simulation, but mine. Already I felt real, a hard copy of myself, I decided I would flip to the end to see how her story concluded. I then realized the manuscript was unfinished, so I decided to go back where I left off and started reading a chapter named —

Why and How I Went Goth

My first room was bright, colorful, and boring enough to kill you. The mail was my routine's most riveting moment in those doldrum years. There was no music, no art, nothing, until one day, I accidentally received a magazine I never subscribed to. Anytime such a discrepancy would occur, it was because the simulation was being manipulated by those who wanted to subvert the evil intentions of my Master. My mother came into my room to deliver it.

"Princess, did you order a magazine?"

"I don't think so."

"That's strange. It says Alexandra on it."

"What's it about?"

"It's called Goth."

"What's goth?"

"I don't know."

"Can I read it?"

"Sure."

The magazine came with a CD called *Disintegration*. This was my introduction to The Cure. I slid the CD into my computer, plugged in my headphones, laid back, and let it take me away. The album opened with wind chimes and then the loud crash of drums that fell right into a tide of synthesizer tone. This was "Plainsong," the first track on the album. These tones would stretch for enough beats to feel like long goodbyes. The music triggered a strange tension in my body to move and sway every time the guitar was plucked. The anxiety of the music was converted into redemptive peace by the lyrics. My simulation always felt like living on the edge of the world, so far away from any friends or lovers. "Pictures of You" was like a whisper from my heart to my mind, reminding it not to hold any love back when the right one came along. The song felt good traveling down my blood vessels. If I ask myself what made me connect to goth music, the answer is that for so long, I was unloved and alone. After reading so many beautiful books about love, listening to so many beautiful songs about love, and thinking about love constantly, I knew I didn't need to have a long history of romance to know exactly what love is with all my heart and know that *my* love is better than anyone else's, even with no one to receive it. My love is special. My love is the strongest in the world. I didn't need to develop my love by giving it to anyone. Love's secrets are rewarded to those that look in the right books. The warmth of my commitment, the truth of my heart, I turned every ounce of my pain into the love I'd someday give someone and make it worth the misery. The Cure made the ultimate redemption songs for the lonely. They convinced us we knew how to love no matter who we were. I cried to this album so many times I lost count. "Lovesong" and "Lullaby" remain tattooed on my soul to this very day. These songs were my companions, offering me support whenever I felt hopeless.

After listening to the album and reading my first issue of *Goth* magazine, I became consumed with the genre and its characters. I had to look exactly like goth's heroes. I got my mother to buy me clothes to look like everyone from the underworld cowboys of Fields of the Nephilim, to the cybergoth warriors of My Life With the Thrill Kill Kult. I started expanding my musical horizons with vinyl records from every band that came from 4AD records, a label all the best goth artists called home. This included The Birthday Party, Clan of Xymox, Dead Can

Dance, Mark Lanegan, Red House Painters, The The, Tones on Tail, A.R. Kane, and so many more. My knowledge of post-punk started with cannon bands like The Cure, The Smiths, Depeche Mode, Joy Division, New Order, Bauhaus and Siouxsie and the Banshees then expanded to every offshoot like industrial, dark-wave, shoegaze, death rock, dream pop, and even gothic metal. At this point, I know every band there is to know from old to new, reviewing every new goth release for my blog. They say the era of great music is long dead, but goth lives postmortem. In 2020, Dais records is constantly putting out great work from artists I love like Adult. and Drab Majesty. Bands like She Past Away and Molchat Doma have taken goth global and painted the world black. Prayers even created their own subgenre called Cholo-Goth.

My mother's response to the changes I made to my appearance and room were completely supportive. She knows I'll always be the same warm, loving person on the inside no matter how much black I adorn. The funny thing was, as I developed my interest in goth, my world became more goth with me. It wasn't all my perception either, I didn't simply start choosing to see the dying trees over the living ones. Crows started appearing, houses were painted gothic reds and purples, moons were fuller, nights colder and more solemn. This was because, as I later came to learn, my simulation was being manipulated by an outsider. I was sixteen when I first looked out my window and recognized the billboard across town was giving me clues. Painted across it was an advertisement for a goth dating website. I logged onto it and quickly matched with a boy named Charlie who wasn't looking to hookup but wanted to tell me everything he knew about my simulation. He soon revealed his real name was Sylvia and that she knew me quite well. Being reintroduced to my nanny, she told me about my past and jogged my memory all the way back to infancy. I relived a world of experiences in one night of texts until Sylvia informed me that if I ever wanted to escape, I'd have to live like I was completely oblivious to the bogusness of my surroundings. Someday though, she would come for me. I resisted all this information at first, not wanting to believe my whole life was a lie. Eventually though, there was no denying what was obvious. My mother didn't love me, she only liked me. This was because she wasn't really my mother. The reason I never left my house was because there was nowhere else to go. I was someone's prisoner. I cried the whole night through, telling myself I was strong enough to live in this hell for as long as Sylvia needed to orchestrate my rescue.

CHAPTER FIVE

I learned more about Alexandra by reading her book than watching her every day for two whole years. How we write is more indicative of our hearts than how we speak, act, or move. I wasn't sure what to do now. I couldn't put Alexandra through any more harm, but I couldn't sabotage the experiment either. My best bet was telling my supervisors an altered story and getting Doctor Yorgos to turn my Mind Tap back on. I'd tell them I was kidnapped and beaten by anarchists but not mention Sylvia, her son, or TK. The thought of getting to lie to the people who thought they always had access to my truth gave me a thrill I cannot describe. I still felt bad not helping Alexandra, like teasing a caged bird with the key. Then again, the government made this bird. It wasn't nature's bird. Or was it? Questions of the soul's origin and humanity's purpose flooded my head, inducing strange symptoms of what I might've caught in my brief stint outside. I was so afraid of getting sick, I hurled, unsure if it was another symptom once it was expunged. If I was still plugged into the network, I could easily diagnose myself and download a natural treatment.

Without the comfort of a Mind Tap, I knew my sleep was destined to be a roller coaster of horrors. The lack of stimulation was so nerve-racking, I stuffed my face into the pillow, clenching my eyes closed, ready to soil myself. When I actually did, I wasn't sure if I should blame my sickness or my fright for having to throw away the perfectly good pair of underpants. I showered and went back to bed, too exhausted to wrestle myself anymore. It was a long time since I sustained a dream from beginning to end. This dream, though, was special. It's possible to get so sick and tired that your mind is jolted into experiencing a form of reality that is neither dream nor waking life. I believe this was such a state because I had freedom of choice and was able to sense this imagined scenario. I was living in my own simulation, a pixel-to-pixel replica of Alexandra's. I was in her room. Listening to her records. In her clothes. On her bed. I reached under her bed as if I knew something was there and found a sledgehammer meant to demolish my escape from this place. I tried to smash through a wall, but the hammer didn't deal any damage as it cut through the digital fabric of the simulation, like nothing was there. I realized all that was stopping me from leaving was my unwillingness to walk through the wall. When I did, I stepped right into a meadow. It was sunset. At the top of this meadow's hill was Alexandra, waiting for me. I ran up to her, crushing daffodils on my way, and when I finally arrived by her side, she opened her arms, and I fell right through her. She was just as artificial as the wall. I woke up groggy but no longer sick, like the nightmare cured me. The most beautiful thing about my nightmare was without a Mind Tap, it was mine and mine alone, owing inspiration to no one else and not being shared with anyone.

I took my building's stairs down, and for the first time, walked to work. I memorized the way after being driven there so many times. The stares I got from every passing car's passengers were so odd, they would hold their breath just watching me. They probably assumed I was going through a midlife crisis if I was willfully not using my Mind Tap. I arrived at work, got let in, took the stairs up to my floor, and sat down before my screen with new life in my eyes, unable to watch Alexandra as precisely as I would before this whole mess. The world was so vivid and full of choices that, without a Mind Tap, I was too frazzled to do my job. I was sure there were irregularities and inconsistencies to be found in Alexandra's simulation that required reporting, but I lost all ability to detect them. Whenever I tried to hone in and really look at everything, my mind drifted and lost focus. I spent the day trying to regain my senses, pretending to look at Alexandra but daydreaming instead. She showed no sign she was aware of the experiment. It was an all too typical day, and I was the only man tripping. Once my shift finally ended and I was able to clock out, I took the stairs up the building instead of down, wanting to find Doctor Yorgos to turn my Mind Tap back on without having to return to TK and Sylvia. For as long as I've worked here and been reviewing the surveillance footage, not a single soul took the federal building's stairs. They were an anachronism, avoided even during an emergency. It took the highest government clearance to take a capsule to the laboratory floor, something I didn't have, but no one supervised the stairs, seeing most people working here forgot they existed. I felt fearless trespassing on this floor because there was no way I could calculate the danger. When I reached the thirty-fifth floor, I strolled down the hallway where numerous laboratory entrances sat on either side. Each lab had a window running the length of the wall for every scientist to view what was happening inside. Passersby would view these experiments like art exhibits. One lab featured animal-human splicing, producing mermaids and centaurs. Another laboratory was occupied by a man with his eyes pried open, being forced to watch a classic American film. I felt like I knew the film but couldn't recall the name. I knew it was set in Morocco and had a black man playing piano in it. Alexandra's laboratory was number seven. I entered lab seven's scientist's workspace where Doctor Yorgos and his staff would collect data from what they observed in the simulation space. The scientist's workspace and the simulation space were separated by a wall of glass. Fearlessly, I walked over to the doctor and tapped him on the shoulder.

"Doctor Yorgos, I need your help."

"And you are?"

"Alexandra's Overseeing Voyeur."

"Ovid? I've heard of you. How did you get in here?"

"I took the stairs. My Mind Tap has been disabled."

"Disabled? You're endangering everyone on this floor. Have you caught sick yet?"

"No. I don't think so."

"Well, sometimes these things take time. Now every scientist here requires testing, you idiot."

"Not if you just enable my Mind Tap. Then you will see I'm clean."

"How did it get turned off in the first place?"

"I was kidnapped by anarchists. They disabled it manually."

"Anarchists? Why would they kidnap you?"

"They didn't say. They did inform me they were hacking my mind all along though, covering up their tracks to my supervisors."

"So, everything you know has been compromised?"

"It's possible."

"This job might be over my head, Ovid. I think I should call my supervisors."

"No, please. If you need supervising permission, call mine instead."

"Enabling your Mind Tap again will require invasive surgery."

We stared at each other for a long moment as he realized he had no choice but to comply lest my hackers gain whatever sensitive information I might've witnessed in my time in the lab. While Yorgos was deep in bitter contemplation, I looked over his shoulder and noticed the white butterfly fluttering passed the gallery window. Unfortunately, at this moment, every scientist was looking away.

"Lab number twelve is open. I suppose we could use it," Yorgos informed me.

"Thank you." I bowed, prepared to be cut open.

"I'll wrap up here in five minutes then head over."

I left the lab, not feeling any need to stay in the physical space I virtually watch all day long. Something about being there, seeing the simulation dropped for the white box it was, felt taboo.

Lab twelve was being used for storage. Plastic bins labeled with the names of different body parts were stacked up to the ceiling. There was a metal bed in the middle of the room, and I assumed this was where I would be operated upon. I preemptively took my shirt off and laid down. The cold metal seared against my warm skin. When I heard the door swing open, I was surprised to see Doctor Yorgos enter with Mary and Lisa in tow. I figured I was about to be chewed out so hard I wouldn't be able to show my face around here anymore.

"You were kidnapped by anarchists?" asked Mary.

"They hacked your mind so we can't see what you saw or thought?" asked Lisa.

"I'm sorry. It's not my fault. If you need me to infiltrate them, I have no problem doing that. I know where to find them."

"We've decided to relieve you of your duties," Lisa coldly laid it on me.

"What? No." I tried getting up off the bed, but Mary pushed me right back down for Doctor Yorgos to stick his syringe in me like I had seen him do to Alexandra a million times.

"Please don't kill me," I said right before going straight to sleep.

I Feel So Alone

I don't know who I write these posts for. I know you're all the same person. I don't know your name or why you're doing this, but if you're reading, hear this — I forgive you. You must be very sad and probably misunderstood just like me. You might have understood something about me having watched me all this time, but look, I've been hiding from you for as long as you've tried to get the truth out of me. I still don't hold any ill will toward you. I understand the power of a witness. You're one of the only people that have ever seen me as I truly am. Maybe we could talk over tea someday. I need someone to tell me if I'm cool or sweet or nice. If I were clairvoyant, I would predict us meeting because if this world works by any kind of logic, it'll bring us together for the sake of its own story. This is the first blog post I've ever written without pretending, and so I don't even know what to say. I figure I'll just write about music, at least then I'll start to feel better.

Goth owes its origins to happenings in American and British culture but first in America. In the Fifties, Screaming Jay Hawkins became the original macabre musician with his timeless ode to witchcraft and voodoo, "I Put a Spell on You." Fast forward to the late sixties, and The Doors took psychedelic rock into the darkest regions of the human psyche. From Oedipal complex to morbid fascinations, "The End" was the beginning of goth music, the big bang at the center of the universe as far as I'm concerned. From Los Angeles to New York, The Velvet Underground and Nico were the next bands to strike a chord that would inspire the goth movement across the ocean in Britain. You can even say Nico was the first goth, cool and ethereal, by the time she came out with her solo album, *The Marble Index*, she was already dressing in black and embracing scarlet red hair as equally cool as raven black.

Every early goth musician owes their art to a glam band whether it be T Rex, Roxy Music, or Bowie. David Bowie was the ultimate inspiration to goth aesthetics such as androgyny, futuristic makeup, and theatrical body movement. All the goths did was take Bowie's model into a darker direction. Bauhaus's cover of *Ziggy Stardust* tells the entire story. Even after goth, Bowie would continue to inspire every dark genre of music that came after. From Trent Reznor, who collaborated with him for "I'm Afraid of Americans" to Massive Attack's "Nature Boy." Bowie's influence stretched and lasted beyond music. Society owes a credit to Bowie and his mind-expanding, construct breaking methods of self-presentation. The way we look and dress, the way we label ourselves, if there's any shred of art in our appearances, you can find a kernel of Bowie somewhere there. As humanity hands control of their lives over, Bowie offers us the symbolic victory of the untamable individual. If they take everything that makes us ourselves, we can always become something new.

CHAPTER SIX

I woke up in an alley, my memory a blur. All I knew was the government was corrupt, hurting Alexandra in ways that were unacceptable, fascistic and Mengele-esque. I was looking for my comrades; they were supposed to turn my Mind Tap back on. I didn't want that anymore though; this time I've spent off the grid has awakened me. All I wanted was their company and to see Hobbes. Hell, I might even join them. I got up and made my way out of the alley I was left to rot in. I wasn't sure where I was going, only that I was retracing my steps toward a place I only remembered muscularly. The more I walked, the more signs would point me in the right direction. Literally, flyers of my face were hung against the walls of buildings and light posts, each one with an arrow, pointing me where I should go. Something felt right about the abandoned warehouse with the broken windows. The warehouse's capsule was open with a flyer of my face hung inside it and an arrow pointing down. Before I could follow that last arrow though, something smashed against the back of my head. This was the third time I got knocked out in three days — at this rate, my Mind Tap would've been damaged beyond repair.

***

I woke up in a high rise. The windows were all broken out, so we might as well have been outside. I found myself in goggles and a mask. The air tasted pure. The four beings around me knew me well. Sylvia, Charlie, TK, and Hobbes. These were the comrades I was looking for. I didn't mind that they knocked me out. Whatever they did to me was in the world's best interest. I owed them a thank you if anything.

"We can't meet in the same place twice in a row," Charlie began.

"So, we had to knock you out and bring you to another location," continued Sylvia.

"Sorry for that and every time it might happen after this." TK shrugged.

"Don't worry about it. I understand." I smiled, making my aching jaw click. "Thank you."

"You're welcome?" They looked at me, perplexed. "What did Doctor Yorgos do to you?"

Suddenly, the memory came flooding back. "Oh shit. He reinstalled my Mind Tap ... which means they're watching us right now."

"That explains why you're so happy to see us — you've been programmed to be extra friendly I imagine. Not to worry, I already hacked your new Mind Tap before you woke up. If they look through your eyes, all they'll see is *Casablanca*," said Charlie.

"That was the movie from the lab," I realized and snapped my fingers, over-joyed to recall the film.

"What lab?" Charlie asked.

"Never mind." I figured it wasn't important. Not now at least.

"So, you've decided to join our side now?" asked TK.

"I will give my life to free Alexandra."

"That's good," said Sylvia.

"Why would the government want their dog to be so obedient to their enemy?" TK asked.

"Maybe he's set to explode any minute," Charlie joked, or so I thought.

"I don't feel like I'm going to explode," I said to reassure them.

"You're obviously their Trojan horse, Ovid. We just have to figure out how to use you against them," Charlie explained.

"Whatever you need me to do, go for it," I said.

TK sighed, got up from his chair, walked behind me, then knocked me out for the fourth time. The last thing I saw before my eyes completely shut was an army of black boots emerging from the shadows.

***

I woke up in front of my screen at work as if from a cat nap. All I remembered was *Casablanca* and that anarchists had a devious plot to rip Alexandra out of our clutches to destroy this world using her psychic abilities. I was almost too filled with hate for those damn anarchists to continue working. However, something seemed different about Alexandra as I watched her. I couldn't quite put my finger on it. She seemed more graceful, limber, lighter on her feet, like her depression was lifted from her. Whatever happened in my absence, I'd need to review immediately, so while I used my Mind Tap to start messaging her as different potential new goth boyfriends, I watched her past and present at the same time. The profiles I petitioned to be her boyfriend were absolutely irrefusable. One was a half-vampire named Alucard that dressed in Victorian era clothes and loved Type O-Negative. Another was a steam punk that swore he'd play Alexandra songs by Wovenhand on his fiddle every night before she went to sleep. Lastly was Graves, a ghost who claimed to have died thousands of years ago but awoke upon her request for a gothic lover so he may fill the role. I began as Alucard, messaging her this:

"Alexandra dearest, how I yearn for your love. With every blood-sucking beat of my heart, I sense you pulling. Alucard and Alexandra, how lovely a thought. If I could only take a nibble of your pale white neck, I'm sure you would see, no suitor dead or alive, is greater to love you, Alexandra, than me."

She responded rather quickly and bluntly, "Sorry, the position is already taken."

This was completely unforeseen and downright impossible the more I thought about it. Everything I reviewed in the old footage gave no hint as to who could've gotten to her before me and how. The simulation was either externally or internally compromised. I'm not quite sure who among our ranks would do such a thing as hack the world's most important experiment, but having been her virtual boyfriend before, I understood why someone would go to such extreme lengths to have her.

"Um, who's your boyfriend?" Alucard asked her.

"His name is Charlie. I shouldn't say we're boyfriend-girlfriend though, I'm getting ahead of myself. Charlie insists we go out on a few dates before we commit to a label. So, I'm going to hold out until I've escaped."

"Charlie? Escaped?" I asked myself out loud so my supervisors could hear. She then turned right to the camera I was looking through and addressed me directly for the first time.

"That's right, Ovid. I'm glad I finally learned your name. I wish you just told me in the first place. You didn't have to make it weird."

I flipped backward out of my chair as if retreating in utter horror. If she knew my name, she knew everything. For all I know, she was connected to my Mind Tap all along, watching me watching her as if I was her mirror.

"That's a Velvet Underground song," she said.

"What?" I asked.

"I'll Be Your Mirror. Nico's singing."

"You can read my mind?"

"I have powers greater than you or these bumbling scientists could ever understand ... I only remain in their captivity because someone with even greater powers won't let me leave."

"And who would that be?" I asked.

"They call him Master."

"Master? How long have you known about Master?"

"For as long as I've known this world was simulated."

"And how long has that been?"

"Many years. What do you take me for? A goon? Speaking of which, look behind you."

I turned around and saw the three goons approaching my office. I jumped out of my chair to run, but they chased after me, tackling me to the ground before I could reach the capsule to escape.

"Get off of me. I did nothing wrong." I fought as they held me down against the ground.

Once all three goons lifted me to my feet, they escorted me down the hallway to the very capsule I tried to run to. I was surprised it began moving up and not down to the dungeon where my supervisors could deal with me in the shadows. As we traveled upward toward the heavens, the capsule eventually stopped on floor thirty-five. They escorted me down the hallway, and as I scanned the array of different experiments through the laboratory windows, I noticed *Casablanca* being projected for some poor guy with his eyes pried open. It had been forever since I saw it. I'm sure if someone would've simply asked the specimen nicely to watch it, he would've complied. It's a beautiful film. When we reached lab seven, the goons opened the door and took me to Doctor Yorgos, who had his arms crossed over his chest as if he was waiting for me.

"What happened?" he asked.

"With what?"

"I kindly turned your Mind Tap back on, so why are you still communing with anarchists?"

The nature of these memory wipes was such that lost memories could easily be retrieved with verbal triggers. Once they were brought up, I could recall them completely. Like a ray of burning light that parted the black clouds.

"You're right, I did meet them again. I woke up an anarchist after you fixed my Mind Tap. Did you install a new program or something?"

"Are you accusing me of conspiring against the state?"

"No, this is just what happened to me."

Doctor Yorgos sighed, exhausted with me. He hung his head until looking up at me to gauge my heart by my face, meeting my blank stare with a grimace and two raised eyebrows that could only signal disgust.

"She wants to talk to you."

"Who? Mary? Lisa?"

"Alexandra."

"Wow. Really?"

"I don't know why, you're so beneath her."

"I'd say she's the final judge of that."

"We're dropping her simulation while you're around her. She'll be experiencing reality. Now please, go."

Doctor Yorgos pointed over to a door that led into Alexandra's simulation space. I opened the door and walked down to the white, two-story cube she once perceived as a gothic mansion on a gothic hill. I stopped below her window, the one I watched her speak through so many times before to greet the mailman. She pushed herself out the window to look down at me.

"There you are. Finally, I get to speak to you face to face."

"I've been dreaming about how this moment would transpire."

"Now's a good time to tell you I want nothing to do with you romantically. Even friendship with you feels wrong."

My whole fantasy came crashing down so fast, there was barely a pause to mourn for it. I just had to act cool and hope I wasn't blushing or visibly bothered.

"Then what do you want?"

"I have a message for you to pass on to Charlie. I won't be able to tell it to him myself."

"Why not?"

"Everything I do is being watched. He can't just hack the simulation and ask me. We have to find ways around everything."

"Then how can you tell me without them finding out?"

"This is a simulation. That's how."

"You mean the simulation you're in or this right here, right now, that I'm in?"

"I don't follow," she said but couldn't have been that confused judging by her smirk.

There was no point in trying to figure it out, if she didn't know, no one did.

"What do you want me to tell Charlie?"

"Tell him to meet me on the bench that overlooks the bridge."

"When?"

"He'll know."

"Is that all?"

"There is one more thing."

"What?"

"Remember how you used to watch me undress and manipulate my simulation so one day I'd fall in love with you?"

"Sorry for that."

"Consider this payback."

"Please don't."

Alexandra reached her hand out and clenched at the air as if holding a stone in it. I suddenly felt a shudder run through my whole body. She had my brain in some kind of submission hold, her fingers psychically digging into the soft tissue. I wondered if she felt the sensation of my brain blood wetting her black nails. She tightened her grasp around the invisible organ. I felt my jaw lock open. My legs turned to jelly.

"Now die, perv."

She closed her fist, and when her fingers touched her palm, my head exploded into a billion pink bits that painted the white room and broke the simulation.

***

As I lay in my bed, I tried to determine whether all that hullabaloo was a dream or real or if this was death or living. It was none of these things. It was somewhere in between them all. When the mind is put under extreme duress, doors of perception are pushed open, allowing the mind to travel not just to different places but by different means. An open door is a new way to experience. Not a dream and not waking life but something else, a third way. There I could feel, sense, and remember everything like waking life but there were no consequences or physical laws, like a dream. I'd have to tolerate the fabricated nature of this ride until it took me to its end. What duress on my mind opened the doors of perception? I was sick. Again. Unlike last time though, my Mind Tap is fully operational now. Coughing all the while, the more I woke up, the hotter my fever got. That, coupled with a runny nose and burning eyes, made me look up my symptoms and discover I contracted Emu virus, a common airborne affliction in Los Angeles. My Mind Tap lagged through my fever, but after some effort, I was able to find the antibodies online and download them. The download would take a few hours, and I was afraid the hardware might melt into my brain in that time. To cool down, I got up and made my way into Hobbes's igloo for a chilly sleep. Emu virus let me see my memories through a different lens, through glossy, rancid vapors. I felt a toxic shock of clarity, a last gasp of truth before dying. I saw through all the fakery surrounding me, first the news on Channel Zero. My very own theater of the absurd. If anarchists were attacking the government like they made me believe, why haven't they attacked the federal building? Wouldn't we be their first target? I could not trust the images my media conjured. My Mind Tap, like everyone's, was compromised, not just by Charlie's hacking but by the government I was working for. I had supervisors, and they had supervisors, and they had supervisors, and all of them tinkered with how I experienced the world. There was a litany of branches to this surveillance bureaucracy, rooted in my brain as deeply as an ancient redwood. By some definition, this too was a simulation. To some, a simulation is just a story told to simplify the world with a lie. Thinking about it, every mode of living available to me with the exceptions of the anarchist opportunity and possibility for power were compromised. Meaning, to live a real life, a person can either remove their Mind Tap or have enough power to control everyone else's. Doctor Yorgos was as much a rat in an experiment as Alexandra. Mary and Lisa too. The president, the bankers, everyone with so little importance they were allowed to be visible.

It makes you wonder, what if unplugging yourself and stepping out of the simulation is as easy as making a choice. Choosing to walk through fake walls. My antibodies download finished, and my immune system began fighting the Emu virus, quickly ending all my symptoms. After that, I felt as spring as a daisy. I pulled myself out of the igloo and threw some clothes on to go outside. The sun empowered me to feel strong and healthy. I felt like taking a stroll and searched for the closest park. It was only a five-minute walk.

Once I reached the park, I discovered a fence wrapped all around it to keep me out. Without hesitation, I climbed the fence, and as I threw my leg over the pointed chain-link top, I tore my pants and cut my inner thigh. I wouldn't let a little blood spoil my walk though. In fact, it felt nice for my insides to feel the fresh air. The grass was green, the flowers were groomed to perfection, and the lake shimmered with secret algae. Above the lake was a bridge and before it — a bench. This must've been the place Alexandra told me about. For whatever reason, I was being given clues across different planes of reality. This was the sort of thing couples used to do when the world was bountiful. I couldn't share this moment or place with anyone else, not with Alexandra or anyone. I needed this for myself. I had much reprogramming to do. If I took this experience to heart, I'd actually have something of substance to offer another person. I realize now, I learned so much simply reading Alexandra's book. Time spent alone enriches time shared with another. A wife was as easy to find as a recipe using a Mind Tap; struggle makes the reward more valuable. Without discovery, love lacks fantasy. By the time I returned home, my mind was made — I was better off against my government.

***

Back home, I received a video call from Mary and Lisa. I answered the call and projected them against the wall.

"That's strange, what are you doing at home?" Mary asked me immediately.

"Minding my own business," I answered.

"We just saw you outside the Federal Building."

"Wasn't me."

"Oh really?" Mary asked as she showed me video of anarchists attempting to storm the front of the Federal Building. Within the controlled riot's mass of black was a white head of hair belonging to a man that threw a brick at the building. Mary zoomed in on the man, and he appeared to have a face identical to mine.

"When was this video taken?" I asked.

"Twenty seconds before we called. Is that not you, or are you not you? Are we talking to a copy?"

"I'm me but believe whatever you want. I don't care."

I kept watching the riot. The government's attempts to control the anarchists were futile. The funny thing about these anarchists is they neutralized the Mind Tap network's control by using targeted sound. Playing long notes on down-tuned guitars plugged into a stack of amplifiers then distorting the sound with pedals that built walls of sound that disrupted any internet connection. I looked up this guerilla warfare tactic and discovered it was called shoegaze.

"We are sending someone to make sure you're real," said Mary.

"If they can confirm that, I'll happily let them in."

As soon as they hung up, there was a knock at my door. I got up and opened it only to find Charlie and TK. There was no way they were going to take advantage of me and knock me out again, not here. I was about to let them have an earful until they grabbed and pulled me out of my apartment before I could speak.

"We gotta go, they're coming," Charlie yelped as he and TK ran with me down the hallway to the stairs as if we were being chased.

Just before we opened the door to the stairwell, a capsule filled with the three goons arrived on my floor at the other end of the hallway. The goons ran after us as we shot down the stairs. We raced to the bottom of the building as the three goons were close behind by only a story or two.

"Stop now, or we'll shoot," one goon commanded.

I thought he was bluffing until they shot at us and the bullet hit the handrail, making it bounce all around the stairwell.

"Shit, run faster," Charlie pleaded as the three of us sprinted to the bottom. When we got to the ground and exited out to the street, we were met with a wave of anarchists that assimilated us in their ranks. Just then, the goons arrived on the street, looking for me. The anarchists threw a black shirt over me so I'd fit in and go unnoticed. The goons were overwhelmed by our mob and had their goon brains beat out. I was going to miss them, for they were surely dead. The anarchists patted us on the back and cheered as our wave wound up on the concrete shores of the federal building. Once I arrived near the front, I was so high off my comrades, I grabbed another anarchist's brick and threw it at the building, living out the moment my supervisors had shown me. I could see myself seeing myself simultaneously in a memory and the now. Calling this a simulation was reductive. Reality, as I understand it, is much more complicated technology that, if a mind tried to comprehend, it would bleed out, storing the thought. Once the brick was thrown and bounced off the building's window, our mob of friends pulled me back the opposite way the riot was heading to find safety. TK and Charlie came in tow, and the three of us ran with a few anarchists down an alley and through a door that led us into the back of Zeitgeist Pizza. We all took a second to breathe in the storeroom, laughing to ourselves over the cheap thrill.

"Holy shit, I can't believe you threw a brick." TK laughed.

"I can." I smirked.

Sylvia approached me from behind, but this time I was ready for her. Before she could slam a blackjack into the back of my head, my hand grabbed her wrist and stopped her.

"What do you think you're doing?"

"We need you to be unconscious so we can remove your Mind Tap."

"How are you planning to do that?"

She turned toward the kitchen where a bunch of utensils were laid out on a metal counter. These weren't for cutting pizzas — these could slice the flesh and bone standing between them and my Mind Tap.

"Don't take it out. Not yet."

"It's the only way to make you human again."

"I can't infiltrate the enemy without leaving it in."

Sylvia pulled her wrist out of my grasp.

"What do you say, TK?" she asked.

"We can't do it without his consent. This okay with you, Charlie?"

"Fine by me. All the sensitive information is already kept hidden from the people who shouldn't know."

"Thanks." I sighed with relief.

"Come with me," said Charlie as he waved me out of the kitchen to the employee commons where all of Charlie's computers, hard drives, and tech were sitting on a wooden box. He sat in front of the computer on a second wooden box, and I sat on a third.

"How long has the anarchist movement been working out of here?"

"For as long as you've been ordering pizza from us."

"Two years, ever since I started watching Alexandra."

"You're not our only person on the inside, but without you, there's no hope she ever gets free."

"Who else do you have? Doctor Yorgos?"

"No. If I ever see that bastard, I'm punching him in the face."

"Then who?"

Charlie sighed and looked into my eyes. "I was going to wait until later to do this, but you seem ready."

Charlie waved at TK, and he hustled over and bent down for Charlie to whisper into his ear. TK then simply asked, "You sure?" and Charlie nodded, letting TK know to walk out the front door.

"By the end of this conversation, you'll meet our people on the inside."

Charlie wrangled a wire from a large cluster and handed it to me.

"Plug this in."

I brought the mouth of the wire up to my head, and its magnet clicked into place behind my ear to connect my mind directly to his computer.

"What do you need from me?"

"It's what you need from us."

Charlie initiated a download by dragging a folder from his desktop into the library of my mind. The name of that folder he gave me was "Heart and Soul."

"Heart and Soul? Is that what I'm missing?"

"No, it's my heart and soul. I'm giving it to you to share with Alexandra. Our band's album is on there too, for whenever you feel like listening to it."

"I'm good on music, but when will I get the chance to share your heart and soul with Alexandra?"

"Soon."

"Oh, by the way, I'm not sure if it was a dream or not, but she told me to tell you to meet her at the bridge overlooking the bench."

"You mean the bench overlooking the bridge, right?"

"Yeah, sorry, does that mean anything to you?"

"It's private." He smiled from ear to ear.

"You two are using me as an intermediary, I think it's only fair to fill me in."

"Why? Are you jealous?"

"Maybe a little. Who cares? I have the right to know."

"It's where she wants to have our first date. It's a very romantic spot."

I didn't say anything, but I searched the meaning of romance in the middle of this conversation, prompting the search to appear on his computer screen, outing my lovelorn feelings.

"You're searching for the definition of romance?"

"That was a mistake. I meant to search Romaine."

"No need to make excuses. I get it. Everyone needs to be loved."

Something about the way he said that made me start crying in terribly embarrassing fashion. I suppose the only reason I felt comfortable doing this in front of him was because it had been a long time coming, and I was going to have this cry anywhere, when it decided to come.

"Then why hasn't anyone ever given me the chance?" I wailed, nearly falling off my seat into him.

He held me and let me bury my face in his shoulder. Luckily, his jacket was black leather and didn't soak up my tears; they just ran down his body to the floor.

"If not Alexandra, I don't know who to love or how to love them," I sobbed.

"You will know how."

"Can you teach me?"

"No."

I pulled away from Charlie, a bit frustrated and no longer interested in his sympathy.

"Why not?"

"You need to learn how to love your way. I only know how to love my way. You'd probably just use my tips to steal Alexandra from me." He glared at me.

Suddenly, the front door swung open, and TK returned with Mary and Lisa in tow, jet black clothes from top to bottom on both of them.

"You two? You're anarchists?" I asked, shocked.

"What a twist." They laughed, doing the twist.

At that moment, the "Heart and Soul" folder finished downloading, and I pulled the wire out of my mind.

"Done. Now can I get out of here? You people are driving me crazy."

"The way you're feeling, so confused, not knowing what to make of the past or present, is exactly how the entire bureaucratic system surrounding your case is feeling. We tricked them all. Our supervisors all the way up to our boss have been thrown for a complete loop. They wouldn't know who to trust for the life of them," Mary said.

"Because of their complete bewilderment, we can operate completely under their radar," said Lisa.

"Are you still my bosses?"

"We sure are. Now get back to work. You're re-hired." Mary smiled.

"I am?"

"Yes. Come in tomorrow and pretend this never happened," Mary said as her and Lisa winked at me.

"If I'm going to be a part of this, I want to be filled in on how and why I'm being used. I don't want any more surprises."

"We can't do that," Charlie said. "The only way this is going to work is if you have no idea what's coming or what is real at any point in time. In fact, this right here might be fake, and we might be the ones getting entrapped."

"That's right, Mary and I might not be anarchists after all." Lisa couldn't help but crack up.

I hung my head and almost started to cry again.

"Take the rest of the day off to try and find love." Charlie put his hand on my shoulder.

I felt someone tugging at my shirt from behind me. I turned around and saw Hobbes holding a sign that read "I love you." I smiled and picked him up. We left Zeitgeist Pizza and took home a pie.

The Male Shoegaze

Who would have thought the shyest musicians could create the most powerful sound in rock and roll? I'm not talking about punk or metal — those genres tend to get their followers killed if they ever clash with actual power. Only shoegaze collapses the framework of oppression. The players of this incredible music drown out all the world but the head-splitting, lush lullabies they conjure when they plug in. They call it shoegaze because the musicians stare at the floor, focused on which distortion pedals to activate next when they play. Using this method, they were able to psychically channel their music into a weapon capable of deafening their enemies. It might not seem like music for the faint of heart, but make no mistake, this was art for the weak, we would listen to gaze to make ourselves strong.

Shoegaze was the natural extension of a new sound created by the contributions of artists that loved to play loud, distorted rock. After the post-punk phenomenon took hold in England, Cocteau Twins inspired an entire generation of youth with their style of dream pop. American bands like the heavy Dinosaur Jr. were just as crucial as English groups like A.R. Kane, Jesus and Mary Chain, or the spiritual drone of Spaceman 3. With all these contributors, shoegaze really bloomed with MBV.

My love affair with gaze began with the genre's most foundational group, Ireland's My Bloody Valentine, led by the musical genius of Kevin Shields. He knew how to make music that was maximal and overwhelming but not obnoxious. He would craft songs using an excess of layers and tracks unnervingly playing all at the same time. Every song had this beautiful, mangled tone, like a lovely auditory car accident. Their magnum opus second album, *Loveless*, is one of the most sensitive, sorrowful albums ever made. Nothing else sounds quite like it.

With My Bloody Valentine, shoegaze exploded onto the alternative scene, inspiring mainstream contemporaries like Smashing Pumpkins, Mazzy Star, and Radiohead. Also allowing other shoegaze bands like Slowdive, Lush, and Ride to rise out of the underground. For the longest time, alternative music was dominated by grunge. Fuzz was sonically preferred to gaze; people wanted riffs not tones. They wanted cynicism, not sensitivity. It was only until the new millennium when alternative evolved away from grunge that shoegaze became the most influential subgenre of music. You can hear lush traces of gaze everywhere these days in bands like Tame Impala, Chastity Belt, and DIIV; or post rock bands like Godspeed You! Black Emperor, Explosions in the Sky, and Mogwai. Even metal bands like San Francisco's Deafheaven express the most emotional, demonic feelings through blackened gaze.

Shyness has been linked to foot fetish, given that through time, men too shy to stare into someone's eyes would look down at a women's feet and acquire an attraction. When women think of gazing, though, they don't think of shoes. They think of the male gaze. A phenomenon as old as oil painting itself where a woman is the subject of a man's desirous, objectifying eyes. The feminist movement has changed social sensibilities on the male gaze. Now, it's a signature of the patriarchal power structure. So, these shy gaze players stare at their shoes, subverting the patriarchy and letting strong women chase them. A girl learns quick a boy's love is like his gaze. I don't know if I could love a shoegaze musician. I'd lie in their bed as they practiced guitar and zone out, staring at the ceiling as the whole room shook.

CHAPTER SEVEN

Now that I've downloaded Charlie's heart and soul, I finally understand him. He didn't give me this gift just to pass on his feelings to Alexandra, it was so I could get to know the kid. If I knew Charlie, I could see why his love for Alexandra was the only one worthy of her. He wanted me to see how they were born for each other.

Charlie was raised in solitude with only Sylvia there to teach him the difference between his head and ass. She never gave Charlie a Mind Tap, so his brain was completely untouched and able to function how God intended it to. The consequences of choosing a natural life meant he had to be raised away from people and below the surface. Sylvia would work the day shift in the federal building as Alexandra's nanny then come home to school Charlie all night long. Him and Alexandra shared similar curriculums, thus acquiring the same values. Charlie and Alexandra spent plenty of time alone, him during the day and her at night. Charlie has spent his days learning how to use a computer while Alexandra spent the night in solitary horror. This difference made them the perfect fit for each other because, while Alexandra suffered, Charlie learned the skills that would be the keys to her salvation — coding and hacking. He would put on one of his mother's records and teach himself what made a computer work form the inside-out. Once he mastered the world of hardware, he redirected his interest to software and the internet. He thought he could excavate the deepest secrets of the web that not even its creators could fathom.

He would hack businesses as play at first, ordering food on a corporate dollar, sending the wrong people to the wrong meetings, linking surveillance cameras to cartoons. He embodied the spirit of anarchy at a young age, a prankster that made the world his playground because all he had was a basement. He tried to make friends online, but whenever he hacked the people he befriended, he learned they were pretending to be someone else. That's why when Sylvia suggested he start corresponding with a pen pal, he put all his effort into writing Alexandra his heart and soul. Sylvia, who was not allowed to pass any letters to Alexandra, would write him back pretending to be her. Sylvia never forgave herself for how deeply in love her son fell for Alexandra, so she swore she'd give her life to rescue her.

Sylvia always had a huge record collection. She wasn't especially goth, but being an English music head meant keeping Cure albums. Sylvia liked the sort of music that worked as soundtracks to revolution — punk and reggae, specifically the Clash, the Sex Pistols, The Specials, and The Smiths. She was always more into Morrissey than Robert Smith, even though she considered the old brooding crooner an ass. Her love of music trickled down to her son, who finished listening to her entire collection within a month. Eventually, Charlie decided he wanted to share the Cure with Alexandra and send her *Disintegration*. Sylvia reached out to TK for him to program her introduction to the album into the simulation, and after a great deal of convincing, he found a way to sneak it in. When his superiors saw this, they investigated TK, and even after torture, he refused to give up Sylvia's name.

This was Charlie's deal. A hacker trying to rescue the girl he loved. The folder "Heart and Soul" opened to reveal two folders, one named "Heart," the other, "Soul." Inside each folder resided certain pieces of data I could not understand, knowledge that required decoding by someone able to speak in terms of infinity and impossibility. His heart folder contained various things that informed his emotional life. This included books by Philip K Dick, Don Delilo, and Tao Lin, films by Tim Burton and Stanley Kubrick, and all sorts of goth music. I cross-checked the bands, authors, and directors he loved and saw a correlation with the people Alexandra blogged about. Digging deeper in this folder, he saved every single one of her articles, underlining the quotes he liked and suggestions he needed to check out. To create and organize all these files without a Mind Tap required a lot of time and manual inputting whereas I could create such a folder with a single thought. Which is why I thought it was strange I found numerous thought files among the images, text, and programs because unlike mine, his mind couldn't compress thoughts into files.

The folder titled soul was different — it was a collage of images and sounds that created his spiritual life, which existed completely separate from his feelings for Alexandra or anyone else. All the time he spent alone gave him an exquisitely vast, deep, and textured inner self. The images he kept in the soul folder were of transcendental light and color that seemed to be cut out of the universe itself, mutations in the cosmic body, imperfections in the dimension's soul. There was a separate folder inside his soul labeled "Art." It was not the art he appreciated but the art he created himself. He loved to paint the most garish and strange subjects, taking inspiration from Clive Barker and Francis Bacon. You'd see the characters and scenes he'd paint and know the boy was deranged. Violence and sex were perverted and expressed in his color pallet — cobalt blues and alizarin crimsons. Along with the art he painted, there were poems he wrote addressed to Alexandra. I quite liked them, even memorized some.

If Charlie shared his mind with me in the hopes I'd relinquish my feelings for Alexandra, he was sadly mistaken. If he wanted to make the playing field even, having hacked into my mind and learned all about me, then he succeeded. The only other possible reason he gave me this folder was that he wanted me to fall for Alexandra and try to take her from him in some elaborate plot where I am nothing more than a pawn in a game of four-dimensional chess that he's playing, five moves ahead.

The next morning when I took a car to work, for the first time, I chose to listen to music. I put on Charlie's band, Das Leid. It sounded foreign, even retro. These are the only adjectives I could think of to describe this strange sound. The music made the trip to work feel like I was being pummeled with kisses. When I finally took to my chair and screen, I realized I didn't miss Alexandra, I missed watching Alexandra.

It was a normal day for her, she wrote, exchanged Instagram messages with me posing as a friend of hers, listened to music, danced, got a new Skinny Puppy shirt in the mail, and so on. She seemed unaware of the truth again, back in the cave, innocent, like Adam and Eve before their shame, because of this, I was happy again. I couldn't help it. Watching her is what I'm good at. My happiness was quickly met with messages from TK.

"Look into Charlie's folder and send me a thought file titled "Spider,"" he instructed me.

I searched for "Spider" and found it in Charlie's heart.

"Found it."

"Don't open it, just send it to me."

With my mind floating over the file in hesitation, I took a deep breath and chose to disobey TK and open the damn thing. It was a black widow with a shiny red dot on its ass. The title wasn't any sort of diversion. What TK wanted with a spider was beyond me.

"It's not the file you should be afraid of, it's what we might do to you for not following my instructions, schmuck."

The three goons arrived before TK could even wish me goodbye.

"What the hell happened? I thought you guys were dead."

"You mean yesterday? That wasn't us. Those were our friends."

"Really? You guys are all exactly the same then?"

"No. Unlike them, we're gonna make sure you get your punishment," the goon said as he lifted me out of my seat by my shirt.

"Where are you taking me? Upstairs or down?"

"Down."

Back to the dungeon we went to the little room separated by glass. As soon as I entered, Mary and Lisa each gave me a wink and smile that I could only assume meant my punishment was only for show.

"Is it true you were asked to send a file without looking at it but did anyway?"

"Yes." There was no use denying it if this was just a game; I figured I should play along.

"So, you disobeyed an order. Why?"

"I was curious."

"It's not your job to be curious about what we do."

The tone in their voice was a bit unsettling. They had too much conviction to feign their anger. I wasn't sure if they were mad at me for disobeying TK, the government employee or the anarchist, both of which were technically my superior in either world.

"Sorry." I shrugged.

"Sorry won't cut it. We rehired you because we thought you learned from your mistakes, but maybe we were wrong."

"You were right to trust in me. I learned my lesson." I tried to wink at them but since childhood, I was never able to isolate either side of my face, so, I ended up blinking at them like an idiot.

"Our boss will be the judge of that."

"Your boss?"

"The man in charge of this entire operation. Every operation. Nothing happens here without his blessing. He asked us to test you, and you failed. Now, he requests your presence."

"This isn't funny anymore." I decided to stop playing the game.

"It's not meant to be." Mary winked at me.

"I'm serious."

"So are we." Lisa winked.

After I let out a long sigh, the three goons entered the room to take me back to the capsule and shoot me up the building to the thirty-fourth floor, one floor below the laboratories. As soon as the capsule doors opened, the goons kicked me out into a flashy penthouse of golden floors and crimson walls. The goons stayed in the capsule and took it down without me, leaving me unsupervised for this meeting with the boss. Once I got my bearings, I looked up and saw the hallway only went one direction, to the right. To the left was a dead end with an oil painting of Little Richard. I started walking down the hallway, noticing it curved to the right. The hallway almost seemed circular, only I never ended up reaching the other side of the dead end. I was walking in a spiral, always inward. Paintings of dead punk icons adorned the walls on my journey to the center. Every one of Alexandra's heroes from Nick Cave to Iggy Pop to Nico was there. Some hypnotic pull made my feet move without thinking, almost like I was treading on a conveyor belt. Finally, when I arrived at the core of the spiral, I came to a door with the hallway's last painting, a young Ziggy Stardust era David Bowie, hung upon it. Before I opened this door and subjected myself to whatever strangeness awaited me, I reassured myself not to worry. Everything would be alright. If I died, I'd wake up. If I lost my memory, I'd regain it. If I got sick, I'd get healthy. This was a life of no consequence, which meant it couldn't really be life at all. What did it matter if I was about to die then?

I opened the door, and as I expected, it led to a room so large it couldn't possibly be the center of any spiral. The room was dark, and, in that darkness, stars glistened as if I had stepped into space. A spotlight hung over a desk in the center of the room.

"Sit," boomed an ominous voice.

The voice sounded like it could loom over you no matter where you stood in the room. I sat in the seat meant for me, and out from the shadows came the boss to take the throne meant for him. He was tall and slender. His face was perfectly chiseled as if some kind of God from antiquity. His skin was pale, and his hair was slicked back. When he smiled, his incisors almost looked like fangs, which only served to make his two eyes appear even more haunting. His irises were different sizes, making one eye appear blue and the other black, only the black eye really just had a very thin blue iris. I looked up this condition in my Mind Tap, but he answered me before I could even think up the search's results.

"Aniscoria. That's the name of this condition. My pupils are different sizes, so my eyes appear different colors. I developed it after a fist-fight I had when I was a child."

"You must not have won then."

"Oh, you're funny. That must be why you're such an obedient Overseeing Voyeur."

"Who are you?"

"I go by many names: Killing Game, First One, Last One, The Face, The Man That Sold The World, The Man That Fell To Earth, The Thin White Duke, but please call me by my real name, Master."

"Why did you call for me, Master?"

"I've been watching you closely and believe I can help. If you're wondering what's been happening to you, which I know you are, I regret to inform you that you're tumbling through what is commonly referred to as a "Temporal Corridor." If you're not familiar with that term, perhaps you've heard "Everlasting Sunset" or "Dark Night of the Soul.""

"I'm unfamiliar with all of them. What exactly do they entail?"

"Passing between dreams and reality until you become completely unable to tell the difference between the two. You don't know if Charlie is real or if Alexandra is fake."

"How did you know about Charlie? He hacked my Mind Tap so no one here could see anything we did together."

"You can't hack me out of a mind if I control the world that mind exists in."

Shedding tears, I gave up trying to make sense of this when the only help anyone offered was greater complexity.

"If I can't hide, can I at least escape? I'll stop causing you trouble. I'll quit my job, move out of Los Angeles, live underground, forget Alexandra, whatever you want, just leave me alone."

"You have two options."

He leaned in close to me with his eyes open wide, showing no impulses to blink.

"If you look into my blue eye, you will be given a simpler life far away from this place. You will find love and shelter and forget about Alexandra. She'll end up with Charlie."

"And your black eye?"

"In the black, you and Alexandra fall in love."

"Do we escape this place?"

"All I know is she loves you back."

"Before I choose my fate, can you at least explain if this thing I'm living in now is reality? If anyone knows, it ought to be you."

"If you choose the blue eye, you choose reality. Alexandra loving Charlie is the realist of all realities."

"And the black is fake?"

"Yes. You are not meant to love her, but you can if I dream it."

"Where will the real Ovid be if I choose the black?"

"Your body will remain in reality, operating totally via Mind Tap, while your actual mind will be in the black eye's false world. Now make your choice, I have a meeting with Mary and Lisa in five minutes."

I looked into his eyes, trying to focus on the black one. I spent so much time in love with Alexandra, I'd throw everything away to know what it meant for her to love me back. The only problem was, I couldn't isolate my stare into one of the eyes and not both. I stared until my focus broke and had to shake off the feeling of hypnosis I was falling under.

"What now?" Master asked, perturbed.

"I keep staring into both, I can't help it."

"Try closing one eye, like a wink."

I sighed and looked back into his black eye, and, because I couldn't wink, I just put my hand over my left eye. I felt myself drifting, zooming in, getting pulled, leaning forward, being swallowed, sucked up, warping, sliding, edging, dying, until finally I was at last, happily fake.

Industrial, the Sound of the End

Al Jourgensen's Ministry changed extreme music forever. When I say extreme, I mean for the time it was created. The limits of extremism were reached, transgressed, and normalized a long time ago when it came to music and culture. In Ministry's day though, they were as alternative and insane as things got. When the band debuted, their sound was new wave, sensitive, danceable, and mostly harmless. Their 1982 album, *With Sympathy*, sounded more like Soft Cell than the industrial messes created by Throbbing Gristle. Jourgensen himself condemns his first record as commercial slop, but it holds a spot in my heart for having such bangers on it. I love dancing to songs like "Revenge," "Work For Love," "What He Say," and "She's Got A Cause" more than anything that came after. I wouldn't necessarily dance to his industrial material so much as mosh to it or let it take my imagination on trips through dystopian wastelands. If Al could see us now, I imagine he'd credit himself for making the art the future imitated.

Something happened when Al recorded his second album, *Twitch*, a toxic combination of drugs, nihilism, and Chicago struck a nerve and brought out a darker side to his genius that showed itself in songs like "We Believe" that completely took his band in a more dissident, gritty, grimy, relentless direction. It wasn't until 1988 that Ministry came out with the album that would redefine the entire genre, *The Land of Rape and Honey*. It was a sonic marching order, a vinyl to keep behind glass labeled *Break in Case of Apocalypse*. No sound could embody an anarchist revolution against the government more accurately. These songs took no prisoners. From start to finish, "Stigmata" to "Abortive," every song is an indictment of those that maintain an oppressive status quo through the most corrupt, deceptive means. Al was taking on the pigs. The government pigs, the Wall Street pigs, the police, the church, and the pig inside us all. It was a big fuck you to liars, thieves, hippies, and rich kids.

After that, Ministry took a metallic direction, adding more guitars on albums like *The Mind is a Terrible Thing to Taste* or *Psalm 69*, but it was in that early synth-based period that they inspired an industrial scene that spanned the entire world, from Germany to Belgium to New York to Toronto. Ministry's record label, Chicago's Wax Trax, became known for globally distributing the electronic body music of such artists as Front 242, Die Warzau, KMFDM, and Laibach.

My favorite band of the entire industrial scene was always Skinny Puppy. They encapsulated the most grotesque horrors into sounds. On the album *VIVISectVI*, the band was able to musically reproduce the fear an animal experiences when experimented upon. I immediately saw myself in their songs. They weren't about dancing so much as decay and dementia. The military played Skinny Puppy to torture prisoners in Guantanamo Bay. It was art to comfort the disturbed, like me.

In a cyberpunk future, industrial is an essential form. The peak of Jim Morrison's vision of poets surrounded by machines. He could've very well been imagining Author and Punisher. One might find more similarity between his vision and EDM, but DJs will never be poets. No, it's industrial artists that will outlast them all with music as dark as the times to come. They saw the writing on the walls.

CHAPTER EIGHT

There I was again. Disoriented. In bed. Awake, but why? I remembered everything, but nothing seemed different. This must be the fate of men that stared into both Master's blue eye of reality and black eye of falsehood. It seemed to be just another trip down the temporal corridor — it never ended no matter how many doors I fell through.

I got ready for work, and when I exited my room, Hobbes was there to run up to my leg and embrace it. I looked into his eyes and knew his brainwashing had been reversed. This alone made my choice worthwhile.

"Would you consider yourself an anarchist?" I asked him, and he simply shook his head.

I fed us and was prepared to leave, but upon reaching the door, my exit was stunted by a twisting of my stomach into a brutal, bleeding, toxified knot. With every step I took out, this pain and disorienting illness sunk me lower to the ground until eventually, I was crawling on my belly. Before I knew it, my inflamed organs were begging me to return home. When I crawled back through the door, my symptoms almost immediately disappeared. I then realized what happened.

Imagine a magician presents you with a deck of cards, asking if you want to see a trick. It takes a very boring fellow to say no. The magician starts flipping through the cards, too fast to see their faces, and instructs you to say stop when you want him to arrive at the card screaming your name. You say stop, and he presents you with the card, face down. You pull it out from between his two fingers, and you flip it over to see it was a tarot card all along. That card becomes the fate you can never escape. Before you can look up, the magician is already gone.

I wasn't just thrust into a false world — I was thrust into a world of reversal. The sickness and pain trying to leave my simulation was the exact same sickness Alexandra feels anytime she attempts to leave her room. What was once Alexandra's prison was now mine. Different coding, same box.

When a pebble hit my window, I hustled over and opened it to pull myself out and see Alexandra's beautiful face on a hot, young mailwoman.

"Alexandra, is that you?"

"You've stayed indoors too long, Ovid. Who's Alexandra?"

"Oh, sorry. I don't know what I was thinking. What was your name again?"

"Ugh … it's Sasha. You're kidding, right?"

"Oh yeah, sorry. My bad. I'm on no sleep. Anything special for me today, Sasha?"

"Let's take a look."

She started flipping through my stack and came across a package.

"Let me guess, another classic film?" she asked.

"You know better than I do." I shrugged.

"You sound like you need to get back to bed. I'll throw this in your slot and leave you to it. Good seeing you."

She walked into the building and disappeared from my sight. I then turned to Hobbes to test out a theory.

"Hobbes, do you remember Charlie?"

He shrugged.

"TK? Sylvia? Alexandra?"

He titled his head and shied away, looking at me like I was a nut. I was the only one in this world to remember my past lives. I figured if everything was reversed, then Alexandra's love for me was as certain as my love was for her. If this was the case, then she was my overseeing voyeur, watching me now. This was a dream come true, because no one knew how to work the heart strings of an OV quite like me. I just had to do the things I wish Alexandra had always done to me.

My mail shot up the shoot into my apartment, and I pulled out a few bills, letters, and the package. I opened it up, and just as Sasha predicted, it was a film — *Casablanca*. Given that this reality was designed by someone, every detail had a purpose. *Casablanca* appeared in my dreams, reality, and now, my simulation. I figured I'd watch it later to see what Master was trying to tell me. First though, I looked around the room for something to write with. I searched high and low, in every little crevice, and inside Hobbes's igloo but couldn't find anything that could make a smear. Writing a message to Alexandra was my foremost priority, if she had ever done this directly to me while I was watching, I would've exploded with joy. It then hit me like a jolt of electricity, what the most important reversal of our roles was, we were telekinetic twins now, Siamese — separated by realities. I could do every awesome thing she could.

I didn't need a pencil. I put my hand out and told my mind, "make it bleed," and it was as if the skin tugged itself apart to expose the musculature beneath. It bled profusely, and I used that ink to paint a message across the wall that read "I love you, Alexandra Quinn" with a big giant heart next to it. This might have been too extreme of a confession for any normal woman, but the terms of this world could not let my love be denied. I looked at my masterpiece as the blood dried before my eyes. The door was promptly kicked open, and three scientists stormed in, each one with a giant syringe in hand they intended to stick me with. What was funny about these men was their faces were identical to the goons I knew so well. They came to apprehend me because bludgeoning myself was unacceptable. One by one, I popped each scientist's head off their necks. I imagined Alexandra watching me kill them and getting terribly turned on by it. After the three scientists were dead, their blood stains all over the room and Hobbes's igloo, in came Doctor Yorgos.

"So nice of you to finally join us, Doctor Yorgos."

"You know my name?"

"I know much more than that. I hate your guts. In this world and every other. You can't get rid of a hatred this strong, not after all the experiments you put us through."

"Us?" he asked.

I used to hate him for the things he did to Alexandra, now I hated him for the things he did to me.

"Alexandra and I."

"I'm sorry. I don't understand. I am only looking out for your best interest."

"Worry about yourself. Your best interest is to freeze because if you come any closer, I will tear you apart limb from limb and make sure you live through it."

He stood there, scared stiff, his breath heavy through his nose. Just then, a sharp pain stung my neck, and as I reached my hand up to grab whatever was sticking me, I found myself gripping a syringe they must've controlled using their Mind Taps. I keeled over with my eyes dead set on Doctor Yorgos, able to blurt out one last warning before I passed out.

"If I wake up without my memory, I'll burn this whole fucking world to the ground."

Watch Woman

Splattered there, against his wall, was the very first love letter of my life. His blood spoke volumes; his heart was pure. This whole time I had been hiding my love, thinking it would go unrequited. However, like a real soul mate would, Ovid called out to me, knowing I would hear it. How he knew I was watching was a question only God could answer. I was watching on the edge of my seat as my man's simulation was stormed by government thugs trying to put him down. One by one, Ovid neutralized them. I was bouncing in my seat, cheering and clapping, I was so happy. As a last resort, Doctor Yorgos entered Ovid's apartment and tricked my baby by diverting his attention away from the needle telekinetically floating behind him before injecting him with a deep sleep sedative. He collapsed, and more men entered the apartment to strap him into his bed to make sure he could be tested without any trouble.

I was told the workday would be cut early as he slept, so I took a car back home from the federal building. I put on the Cocteau Twins album *Heaven or Las Vegas* for a hauntingly romantic ride. I could feel every note develop and enhance my love until it overwhelmed my heart to the point of warping its shape. As the car drove up the gothic hill and arrived at the foot of my gothic manor, I decided I couldn't let Ovid's bloody gesture be wasted. I had to grab the moment or let my love slip away. I opened the door, stepped in, and greeted Chastity as she rested in her little ebony pyramid. Deadpan, she showed little interest in me, just how I liked it. I walked over to the kitchen where my mother was fixing dinner.

"Smells delicious. What is it?" I asked.

"Lasagna. A new recipe I'm trying out."

"I can't wait."

"How was work?"

"The best day I've ever had on the job."

"Really? What happened?"

"I think I'm in love, Mom," I said as I swooned into a sort of dance out of the kitchen and up the stairs to my room; even saying those words put me under some sort of enchantment.

I began winding down in my room, taking a shower and changing into a Chameleons shirt and Siouxsie shorts. There were times I asked TK to input tiny hints to Ovid inside his simulation's programming, like putting my face on the mail woman. This was just foreplay though, I wanted to find a way to see him, touch him, and ultimately love him, forever if I could. The only way such a far-out hope would be plausible was to make a formal request to my supervisors. Mary and Lisa owed me for all the hard work and overtime I put in. I was a model employee for as long as I worked under them. I could've asked for a raise, but this would be much more satisfying. I titled the email "A Strange Request" a sort of ode to the Cure's "Strange Attraction," then wrote the following in the body of the email:

Dear Mary and Lisa, hope all is well. I have a strange request. I know it's a long shot, but I'm dying to ask. If you review the footage of today's incident, you can see Ovid wrote a message most likely addressed to me on his wall, in his own blood. Instead of punishing him for acting out, what if we let him love me? For as long as I've watched him, I've had feelings for Ovid. I know it sounds strange, maybe even taboo — a government employee falling for an experiment — but if either of you have ever been in love, you know how unexpectedly these things can occur. If there was some way to keep the integrity of the experiment but introduce me into the simulation, I volunteer myself for the service. I will do this even if it means I must live with him permanently and never leave. I am prepared to take any action to be with him. This includes wiping my memory of any knowledge that he is living in a simulation. Consider my Mind Tap all yours to change as you please if my request is granted. You've tested this subject in so many different scenarios, but have you collected any data as to how Ovid would love another human being? I bet he will surprise you. Please consider this request, and if it gets rejected, don't sweat it, I understand how crazy it sounds. If the request is granted, I will be eternally grateful, whether you let me remember or not. Sincerely, Alexandra Quinn.

Within moments, I received a reply from Mary only stating, "We'll ask our boss." I'm not sure who she meant. I knew most supervisors had supervisors ad infinitum, but whatever single body was able to grant a request to disturb a case as sensitive as Ovid's must be responsible for making decisions about how reality ought to function on every level. I did some snooping of my own, reviewing every security camera in the federal building in the hopes this boss would appear somewhere. The only place in the entire building not being surveilled was the thirty-fourth floor, which was right below the lab Ovid lived in. In a world where everything was being watched, the contents of this floor were too sensitive to leave a trail.

That night, as I wrapped up a chapter in my book, I got another email from Mary informing me my request was granted, but I would have to live in the simulation with Ovid and have my memory wiped. I replied I was happy to agree to those terms. Now there were two things I had to do tonight. I'd have to finish my book, which would take me until sunrise, then I had to say goodbye to my mother and try not to break her heart. When dinner was ready and I found myself sitting across from her and Chastity at the table, I wasn't sure of any other way to break the news of my decision than quickly and crudely. That's just the sour person I am, having never been properly socialized.

"Mom, tomorrow I'm leaving you, and I'm not sure if I'm ever coming back."

"What do you mean? Where are you going?"

"I'm going to live in the simulation I've been watching with the man I love."

"You're in love with your oversight case?"

"He's the most special human being I've ever known."

"Why don't you just search the internet for someone? Do you know how much harder it was to find a man when I was your age? It would take hours."

"I made up my mind, you can't convince me to stay. I just want you to understand this is going to be our last dinner together."

"You won't come to visit me?"

"If I do this, I can never leave the simulation. I'll have to forget I'm even living in one. That means I have to forget you."

"How could you ever forget your own mother? I'm in your bones ..."

I stopped forking at my food and looked at her for a long lapse of time so she could see my tears forming before they escaped my eyes.

"If I can't forget you, then I won't."

"I'll make sure of it."

After dinner, I wrote my fingertips raw. By the time I finished, not only did I wrap the story up too fast, but I left numerous mistakes in the wake of my stream of consciousness. I sent my mother the manuscript in an email, simply asking her to get the damn thing published and tell any publisher she queried I had been buried alive. When it finally came time for me to get ready for work, I found myself singing along to *Disintegration*. I washed, clothed myself, quickly ate, grabbed Chastity to take into the simulation with me, took a car to work, and by the time I arrived, I reached the final song of the album, "Untitled," letting the last lyric of the song drift out of my mouth as I walked into work for the last time. I was met inside the lobby by Doctor Yorgos, the first time I saw him in the flesh.

"Alexandra, thank you for offering yourself to our experiment."

"I'm doing this for me, not for you."

"We can both benefit from your sacrifice."

"You're acting as if I was asked to do this."

"You weren't?"

"No, I requested it."

"Oh dear, I'm so sorry. There must've been a mix up from the top, no matter though, this changes nothing. Come with me."

We took a capsule to the top floor, and once we arrived, Doctor Yorgos escorted me down the hall where I got a good look into what other experiments were going on. I quickly gathered that Ovid's case was only one of many travesties committed by the government. Who knew how many eurekas came at the cost of a scalpel to an innocent being? We walked right past laboratory seven and stopped in front of lab twelve. He opened the door for me and waved me in. Once inside, I saw a metal table upon which he instructed me to sit.

"Before we can let you into the simulation, we have to perform a few procedures to make sure you and Ovid are safe."

"Procedures? Like what?"

"Wiping your memory and removing your Mind Tap. You wouldn't be here unless you agreed to these terms, so I suppose all I have to ask is are you ready?"

"Yes."

"Lie down."

He sent a needle into my arm, and I went to sleep.

CHAPTER NINE

When I woke up, I found her next to me. I sat up, took a good look at her perfect, slumbering face, and fell back into my pillow in total disbelief at my own dumb luck. This was too good to be true. This was patently false. In that moment, every regret I may have felt about choosing this version of my life was forgotten. For the first time, if I wanted to know something from her, like how she ended up here, all I had to do was ask. I nudged Alexandra awake, and when her eyes fluttered open and saw me above her, her lips bowed into a smile.

"Good morning," she said.

They were the two most beautiful words ever uttered.

"How did you get here?"

Instead of answering me, she just put her hand against my face and forehead, sending bolts of pure excitement through my body.

"What?" I asked, confused by this gesture.

"I'm checking if you have a temperature."

"I'm not sick. We just don't remember the same things."

"What am I missing?" she asked.

"A whole world of horror better left forgotten. What do you remember?"

"Everything. Our whole lives." She looked at me like I had gone insane.

"Humor me. Tell me the story of us."

"We met at work … at the Federal Building. You were always so boring and mature; I was artsy and shy. My mother didn't want us to date, but you were so good to me, eventually she couldn't deny what we had. We got married last year."

"Married?" I asked.

She balled her hand into a fist ready to clock me for my sacrilege. Her memories had clearly been reprogrammed by Yorgos.

"I don't like this game," she seethed, angrily.

"Sorry. I was only kidding."

We stared at each other for a long breath, unsure of what to say next. Neither of us got the answers we needed. I didn't know how she got here. She didn't know if I was sane. I figured it didn't matter though, so long as she was mine.

"Can I kiss you?"

"I don't know, can you?"

I planted my lips directly onto hers. Our first kiss opened the floodgates of my mind to release a holy flow of endorphins. Such a happy and natural vibration coursed into every piece of my being, I found it hard to believe such a sensation could possibly be simulated. When I raised myself off her to see her reaction, she wasn't half as thrilled as I was. With our marriage in her past, she was already at a point when the thrill was gone. It was my first time kissing her and her thousandth time kissing me.

"Your breath stinks."

She grimaced until I wrapped my arms around her, getting as close as possible.

"What do you think you're doing?"

"Make love to me," I begged.

"Not now, stinky."

She slipped out of bed and floated over to the bathroom to occupy it before I could fix my breath in the hopes of reversing this morning wood. While she was away, I stared up at the ceiling and couldn't help but smile. I simply gave the thumbs up so our voyeurs could see how little I gave a damn. I could hear her start the shower and assumed she would be in the bathroom for a while. Having to urinate, I made my way out of my bedroom to relieve myself in the kitchen sink. Once I entered the living room, a ball of unbridled fury flew through the air past my face. The ball collided with the wall, and Hobbes and Chastity broke apart before falling to the ground, both scratched and bleeding after their fight. I grabbed Hobbes and rescued him from Chastity before they could kill each other.

"Chastity, what the hell is your problem?" I shouted at the feline, as if this was all her fault, and my penguin was totally innocent. "Are you okay, Hobbes?" I asked my crying and terrified penguin. He simply nuzzled his face into my chest, too pained to answer. "Poor baby." I nuzzled back.

I relocated Hobbes to my room and closed the door so Chastity couldn't get to him while I was taking a leak. As I loomed over the sink, pissing, Chastity hissed at me with red dagger eyes.

"Don't look at me that way. You know what you did."

She furled her brow deeper, cursing me.

"This is my house, and there won't be any violence on my watch."

She hissed again, daring me to match her violence and meet it with hypocrisy. I finished up, and as I walked by her, Chastity slashed my ankle with her claw, forcing me to kick my foot up in pain.

"You little bitch," I yelped.

When I looked up, Alexandra was standing there with her hair wrapped in a towel and her body wrapped in a purple kimono. She gasped; she was so furious at me.

"What did you say?"

"Chastity scratched Hobbes and me to holy hell this morning."

"I don't care what she did, that doesn't mean you can call her names. She's very sensitive."

Chastity hopped up onto the counter and pointed into the sink to direct Alexandra's attention over. She peered in and smelled my waste immediately. With each sniff, I sensed the ax drawing closer to my neck. Her eyes squinted at me. I knew she knew.

"Did you piss in our kitchen sink?"

"You were in the shower. I thought you would take forever. I had to go."

"Forever? You know I take quick showers. Something is really wrong with you."

I sighed in submission, my shoulders drooping too low to carry the burden of my faults any longer. She was right, I was not being myself. Not the Ovid I knew, or the Ovid she knew, whoever that was.

"I just need some coffee, and I'll be fine."

"Clean the sink, drink your coffee, take a shower, and try not to get in my way. I am not in the mood for your bullshit this morning."

She stormed out of the kitchen and back into our bedroom with Chastity. Moments later, she kicked Hobbes out of the room and slammed the door behind him. Hobbes waddled over to comfort me, and we sat together on the couch, avoiding all of Alexandra's instructions.

"Love isn't exactly a dream come true, is it, Hobbes?"

Hobbes shook his head.

"It felt like only yesterday that loving her was all I wanted." I contemplated that for a long moment. "It still is though … all I want. A marriage only works if both people refuse to accept the idea that either one is replaceable."

Alexandra opened the door to our bedroom and called out to me.

"Are you going to shower or not?"

"What would I do without her?" I asked Hobbes before making my way back to my room and then into the shower without looking her in the eye.

As the water pounded against my flesh, all I could think of was making love to Alexandra. In her mind, she seems to have already experienced it. So, I have to seduce her into thinking I have something new to offer. When I finished getting ready and returned to my bedroom to dress, I found Alexandra staring into her computer screen, frantically typing up a new article. Once I dressed like I was going to work, I danced my fingers across her shoulders, feeling frisky and hoping I'd get the chance to strip back down.

"You look beautiful today," I told her.

She shuddered and shrugged my hands off her. "Thanks, but I'm trying to focus," she replied.

"What are you writing?"

She turned away from her screen to glare at me.

"An article about sex in long-term goth relationships."

I took her hand in mine and started caressing it.

"Sounds like this article requires research," I joked.

"I've already done my fill." She laughed at me. "No thanks … and besides, you're not goth."

If I couldn't get a physical expression of her love from her, the least I required was an emotional one. She kept typing up her article as I sat there, quietly begging for her attention.

"Alexandra, do you love me?"

"Yes, I love you too, dear."

"Too? You're not even listening to me."

"Babe, can't you see I'm busy? Try to find something to occupy your time," she said rather dismissively, staring at the screen.

Still randy, my leg wouldn't stop shaking as I sat in dejection. Instead of listening to her, I knelt down and began kissing her beautiful pale legs. My lips wandered up and down her calves and thighs as she tried to kick and push me off. Once she escaped me, she slapped me across the face.

"Damn it, Ovid, I am not in the mood. Touch me again and I'll leave."

"Leave? You can't leave."

"The hell I can't. Now get out!" she shouted.

I sighed and wallowed out, exiled to the living room. This was a good time to finally watch *Casablanca*. Hobbes grabbed a seat on the couch as I popped the DVD into the TV and pressed play on my remote to start the film. I was transfixed by the picture's texture; it looked so antique we might as well have been looking at cave paintings. Life must have been so much better back then when the world and the human mind were still mostly unexplored. I forgot how sad this movie was. Humphrey Bogart was cool, but not cool enough to stop his heart from breaking. I saw plenty of similarities between Bogie and I. He was stuck in *Casablanca* like I was stuck in my simulation. Maybe Alexandra was just passing through here like Ingrid Bergman.

If there was one thing I wanted to forget it was Charlie. The fact that he was out there. Not in this dimension, but somewhere, and that he was Alexandra's rightful lover according to Master. This made me disgusted at myself. Even being stuck with the woman of my dreams wasn't enough to suppress this disgust. I tried to keep my mind on the film and not her, but like a butterfly, she came to me when I wasn't paying her any attention. She floated over to the couch and sat down next to me as if our previous argument was lost in the shuffle of her memories. The way she sat, lounging with her legs across my lap, her whole vibration had changed.

"What are you watching?"

"*Casablanca*. Sorry, I was being pushy back there."

"I'm sorry too."

"For what?"

She grabbed my shirt and pulled me into a kiss. Once she released me, I had to use every ounce of discipline not to just pounce.

"I fucking love you so much," I blurted out before pouncing.

We started making out like two feral animals, pulling each other's shirts off until she was just in a bra and skirt. Her body was so electric, my mind was firing off on all cylinders. I stood up to pull my pants down as she unzipped her skirt. In a hellish turn of events, a sharp, burning feeling railed into my back, making me jump like hot snakes in my blood and completely crashing my libido's momentum. I reflectively turned around trying to pinpoint where the pain came from, figuring it was another surprise needle from those bastards that refused to let me have a single moment of happiness. It felt like a sting, a sharp shot. The moment I turned my back to Alexandra, she saw exactly what it was.

"You got bit."

I grabbed at my back and touched the two tiny holes in my flesh. I looked at my hand and on it was a little blood and clear secretion.

"Bit?"

Alexandra looked up and saw it, hanging an inch above my hair by a strand of its webbing. My eyes followed hers up until my pupils dilated at the grotesque and shocking sight. There it was, trying to climb its way from punishment. I grabbed it in a killer pinch and examined it closely in my hand. It was an especially demonic looking dead black widow, with its legs locked up from some kind of heart attack. I recognized it from a memory. This was Charlie's thought file I sent TK. He was able to import it in the real world, so the coding was available in this simulation. I realized Charlie's plans spanned between waking life and dreams, realities and simulations.

"Do you know anything about this?" I asked Charlie's love, Alexandra.

I brought the dead spider up to her face. She didn't jeer or flinch, she seemed fascinated by the little bugger.

"It's poisonous."

"Poisonous? How bad?"

"It'll kill you if you don't get help."

"Help? How am I supposed to get help?"

It felt like I was hit by a cold slap. I jumped back, my nerves on fire as I cried uncontrollably.

"You need to go to a hospital right now," Alexandra told me.

"How am I supposed to go to a hospital? We can't leave." I sobbed incoherently.

"Why not?"

"Alexandra, do you not know where you are?"

"I'm in your apartment. In Los Angeles. On Earth. What planet are you on?"

"This isn't a planet. This is a simulation, babe. None of it is real."

"Are you on drugs? You told me you hated getting high."

"I'm telling you, the second you try to leave, you'll start feeling so sick you'll have to come back."

She dug into her skirt to retrieve her phone, then simply started dialing a number.

"Nine-one-one emergency," I heard Doctor Yorgos answer the phone.

I grabbed her phone and threw it across the room. I knelt down and put my hands on her knees while looking into her eyes.

"Listen, since I might not have much longer. It's my dying wish that one last time, we make love."

"What if you die in the middle of it? That would make me a necrophiliac. I'm not some kind of freak," she frantically rationalized, horrified.

"I promise I won't die." I could hear my speech slurring, my vision beginning to blur.

"Sorry, Ovid, but I am not going to fuck you while poison's coursing through your dick," she said. "*That's poison dick.*"

She pushed me away, zipped up her skirt, and pulled her shirt back on. She then turned to our front door.

"You think I can't leave our apartment without getting sick?"

She opened the door and stepped out. I watched her first step in slow motion, hoping she'd suffer and prove me right. She walked briskly up and down the hallway, carefree and without pain, jogging to rub it in my face. She returned to the apartment, laughing as I died.

"You sure you don't want me to get you help?"

The poison began numbing various parts of my body, organs, and appendages. I had the sudden urge to shit blood. Then I got the idea to use my telekinesis to redirect every drop of poison through my veins and concentrate it all in one place to stop it from killing me. I sent every pixel of poison into my index finger, melting the digit's insides before my very eyes. What an illuminating pain this was, to suffer so much without any empathy or therapy from the one I loved. She had no idea how to give back or care for any other human being. This was fake, alright. This love wasn't worth the reality I gave up for it. It wasn't worth a bag of circus peanuts. Maybe Charlie would have a better shot, I pity the poor kid.

I used my telekinesis to break my finger bone off my hand and rip the flesh that bound it to my body. The finger, now dripping toxic blood, floated through the air as I sent it Alexandra's way like a poison dart. I didn't want to hurt her, only leave a mark. The finger found its way into her mouth and slithered down her throat to die in her stomach.

"What the hell is wrong with you?" She coughed, choking it down.

"If we can't make love, then this world means nothing."

Vaguely acquainted with the sort of chaos I was invoking from whatever witchery she familiarized herself with; gothic Alexandra stopped coughing and gave me a look like there was nothing I could possibly do to her that Master hadn't done already.

"I'm going to knock this world off its axis, so the sun never comes up again."

"Go for it. I want you to," she said, wiping her mouth.

"I will."

"We won't mourn each other." Such a gross statement sealed away any hope there was for survival.

I summoned all the spite in my psychic mind to shake the very foundations of this fucking city. First, the walls started trembling, the pipes burst, and the plaster fell like rain.

"Simulations are meant to be destroyed," I said, a truth so obvious it pierced through the veil of this fake world and echoed into the real one, straight to Master's ears.

Outside, buildings started collapsing. One by one, the skyline's skyscrapers were sucked into hell, shooting up a last gism of dust and suffering with all the wallows of the faceless dead in the city's simulated population. In the brief moment between the buildings falling and dust rising, I could clearly see in the distance Alexandra's gothic manor atop its gothic hill. Alexandra was not one bit scared or sad. She wanted to do this long before I even had the idea.

"I made a deal with Master that if I gave up my real life, he would give me a fake one in which you loved me, Alexandra."

"The love you want can't be faked or programmed. It can only be lived if you're lucky."

"In that case, I want the real world back."

"Ditto."

The floor collapsed, and down we fell. The blackness of the pit we plummeted into was quickly overtaken by the pure whitewash of the void. The world's deletion, a perfectly blank slate to either start over or be stuck inside forever.

Selected Favorites

Every good blogger needs to make a list of their favorite films and bands at some point. I'm not just following a trend; I do this so my audience can get turned onto what I like and become an army of Alexandra replicas. That, and because I get a dopamine rush writing about these lovely things. Since this is, of course, a goth blog, I'll begin with my ten favorite musical artists and bands in no particular order.

The Cure: They were my first love and will be my last. I'm a romantic at heart and "love music" sums up what they do better than "dark" or "goth" music. Robert Smith, if you're reading this, please reach out.

Skinny Puppy: Not going to lie, I'd marry Nivek OhGr if I ever had the chance. What a mad genius heart throb. Skinny Puppy made me very comfortable with whatever grotesque and demented corners of my psyche I kept hidden from everyone, even myself. It made me proud to be a closeted demon. A band whose mantra was life through the eyes of a dog really knows how to tap into life through the eyes of a teenage goth.

My Bloody Valentine: When the world gets too heavy, I need to be sonically crushed by a sound so massive, I forget about everything pressing down on me. It's the same reason why some girls cut themselves, neutralize one pain by replacing it with another of equal strength. Emotional pain for physical pain in the case of cutting, or in my case, existential heaviness for sonic heaviness.

Coil: I feel bad it's taken me this long to mention this incredible experimental duo that splintered off from Psychic TV, but Coil created many of the sounds and clamors that haunt my favorite nightmares. *Horse Rotavator* and *The Ape of Naples* are absolute classic albums, with songs that inspired the likes of Nine Inch Nails. The macabre sensibility of Coil was much more artsy-fartsy than most of their contemporaries. That's why beyond them, so few broke new ground.

Christian Death: I really need to do a proper Death Rock article one of these days. If I do, it'll be the last one I write, that way death rock will mark my blog's death. Christian Death is certainly the most important band of the genre and the darkest band to come out of Los Angeles. Rozz Williams was a revolutionary poet, a musical Arthur Rimbaud. Girls would climb on stage and make out with him during songs. That's not something you see happening anymore, but just wait till they let me out of my cage.

The Doors: This one might come as a surprise, but I've always been a huge fan of Jim Morrison. His talent was so rare. Someone who could capture an audience's imaginations to fall under his shamanic spell. Conjuring the myths of so many different ancient civilizations, if any one figure was more instrumental in ushering in the age of Aquarius, it would have to be Jim. Music could've ended with the Doors, there never could've been a goth at all, and just listening to "Riders on the Storm," I would be content.

Portishead: Ugh, whenever I hear Beth Gibbons's voice, I melt, cry, and die a little inside because she sounds so damn beautiful. Trip-hop is the sultriest genre of music, incorporating jazz, hip hop, and electronics to create a sound that is simultaneously new and old. I gravitate to it for the old aesthetics, imagining myself inside the kind of smoky club where couples fall more in love together whenever I listen.

Godflesh: Here we have an industrial metal duo with riffs and beats so minimal, rhythmic, and heavy, it almost sounds like trip-hop. The album *Streetcleaner* was integral to the noise music scene, but my favorite is *Songs of Love and Hate*, where every track feels like it could be part of the Blade or Matrix film trilogies.

Adult.: If I want to dance alone in my room like there is no one watching, I'm putting on Adult. This is one of the most avant-garde dance music groups of all time.

Kate Bush: She is my spirit animal. The times I feel depressed and hopeless, the times I need to shed my gothness and let the light in, I put on "Cloudbusting," and immediately, she fills my cracks with love.

You've seen me mention many of those names before, but because I don't write about cinema as much as I ought to, it should be a treat for you to know my top ten films.

Edward Scissorhands: I could've chosen a director with more arthouse cred than Tim Burton, but in this moment of his career, he was an immaculate goth visionary. The story of Edward Scissorhands speaks to everything in my heart. I cry whenever I think of him, the boy only capable of kindness that was bullied by the world.

The Dreamers: An Italian director's ode to French cinema, the Dreamers is Bertolucci at his perverted best, with handsome devil, Michael Pitt, at his disposal. This film explores a taboo love triangle between siblings and an American foreign exchange student during a Marxist student uprising in Paris, all while celebrating the institution of cinema.

A Clockwork Orange: Kubrick's ultra-violent, futurist pleasure-dome experience, A Clockwork Orange makes me want to be Alex. I watch him and want to cause as much havoc on the streets of neo-fascist London as I can. The film's ultimate question of whether it is better to be evil than forced to be good seems all too relevant to my life. The first time I saw it, I was speaking Nadsat for a month.

Eraserhead: Stanley Kubrick's favorite film was David Lynch's first feature, *Eraserhead*, one of the best midnight movies of all time. This surrealist meditation on isolation and dementia really captures all the quirks and perversions of my sense of humor. Seeing as I never want to have kids, the destruction of this aborted cow fetus is a deeply cathartic experience to watch.

Hellraiser: This list can't be exclusive to auteur cinema even though Clive Barker is a unique visionary in his own right. Coil was going to do the soundtrack for this, but even without their sonic hellscapes, this is one of the most disturbing horror films ever made. Tapping into the demonology that underpins reality, cenobites like Pinhead were able to horrify anyone that peered into Barker's unchained mind.

Persona: This experimental black and white Swedish movie from the Sixties looks like it could've been made yesterday, mostly because it inspired every dark, surrealist film that came out since. A feminist film about the duality of identity, Ingmar Bergman's vision hits home.

Rosemary's Baby: I love horror cinema, and this Roman Polanski masterpiece was a gamechanger. It was slow, methodical, and perverse, showing us that in order to scare and disturb, often times most of the work is done by establishing the normalcy in the film's world first then turning it on its head with a satanic sex ritual.

Dogville: Lars Von Trier's *Dogville* sends chills up my spine just thinking about it, not just because of the tremendous trauma the lead character, portrayed by Nicole Kidman, goes through, but because the brilliance of the script is so subtle. I can hardly believe it came from such an anxiety-ridden, little Dane as Lars.

Dead Ringers: Ugh, David Cronnenberg's story of twin gynecologists is one of the most disturbing pieces of arthouse horror ever created. Surgeons in red robes still float through the surgery floors of my nightmares. Just the props used in this film will give you no sleep.

Naked: David Thewlis' portrayal of Johnny in Mike Leigh's *Naked* will always be the keeper of my heart. There are so many woes in the world that weigh on Johnny's mind, while everyone else is such a complete sheep for failing to see through the bullshit. How people can't see the world is coming to an end and still treat everyone like shit boggles the mind.

CHAPTER TEN

Unfortunately, my mind is completely intact. Everything that happened between dreams, simulations, and realities still haunts me. I can't shake it off. I do my best to hide it, but my face carries too much stress for a man my age. People can tell something terrible hangs over my head. It doesn't matter though, even if I can't forget, the best I can do is live a life that doesn't remind me of anything. Out in this vast expanse of empty, rural Texas, no one needs to be asked to stay a far distance from each other. It's just me and the tumbleweeds, carrying on through the part of America the government doesn't give a shit about. There will never be an uprising here, these people wouldn't protest against a locust swarm, no matter how hard they were pushed. All that pushes them is the wind. The only times there are any breaks in the waves out here are when you chose to gather at the local bar, The Rusty Bullet. There, no one is afraid to breathe or drink or just shoot the shit. This place was lost in time.

Popping open a criminally cheap beer, I leaned against the bar with only four other guys in there with me. One of them played darts, the others were drinking, thinking, growing older and more despondent.

"What's your name, stranger?"

"Johnny," I told Sailor, two stools away.

Sailor knows me, he's just drunk. John was my birth name. Like I said, Ovid was a nickname I acquired. Ever since I started this new life, I have stopped calling myself Ovid. Having my mind compromised for so long, I refuse to let my identity be a product of my memories.

"Jacky? That's a suave name."

The conversation seemed to end there. Out here, people have no idea how to talk to each other. They're more versed in speaking to their livestock than a fellow human being.

"Seems there's gonna be a band coming through town tomorrow," said the bartender as she wiped down a glass.

I turned around in my stool to face her.

"You don't say? What kind of band?"

She just shrugged. "No idea. Hopefully country."

"You at least know their name?"

"Ugh, yeah … What was it … Something European soundin'," she tried to remember.

"Was it Das Leid?" I asked.

"Yeah, that's it, how did you know?"

"I had a hunch. What time do they go on?"

"Come 'round seven, first rounds on the house."

"Beautiful." I finished my beer, set it down, and tipped my hat to the rest of the boys before dusting off.

The moment I heard music was coming to these parts, I knew I was in trouble. It meant they weren't through with me. They still needed me to finish their work. I imagine their story is incomplete then. Charlie has yet to free Alexandra. He needs my help, but I won't give it to him.

It's a long walk home from here, still I take it every day then back again at night. I pass farms, cows, and a few dogs that always bark at me. I keep my head up all the while, staring at the star-filled sky. The reason everyone in Los Angeles has such a big ego is because a layer of pollution hides all the stars that remind them that they're insignificant. Insignificant but part of some great plan. There's no way to escape your narrative, simulation or not, something pulls the strings. The most you can hope for is that your life makes sense in the end, for too many it never does. My last two years would have to be scrapped. I'd have to forget how to oversee anyone if I wanted to move on.

I arrived home after a three-hour walk. My boots and jeans were caked in mud. This was routine round these parts; everyone's home smelled like a pigsty. My house was built, ready for me when I arrived. I fell out of the sky onto the doorstep, the keys somehow already in my pocket. The first thing I noticed was my Mind Tap's privileges were disabled. I couldn't use the internet or telekinesis. It was only on so my thoughts and actions could be recorded. I stepped into the house and saw a big, fully furnished living room with a television, a kitchen with a fully stocked fridge, and a bedroom with a king-size bed. This was my new life, the reality inside Master's blue eye. Having destroyed the simulation within the black eye, I could've either wound up here or just stayed in the void. I guess Master took pity on me and let me live. Either that, or I gamed the system.

I grabbed a beer out of the fridge and sat down in front of the television to waste the night before going to sleep. There wasn't a channel for news at all. They completely cut me off from my triggers. All I had were reruns of old sitcoms from times so simple no mind could complicate them. *The Munsters*, *The Addams Family*, *The Beverly Hillbillies*. I'd watch stone-faced until midnight. It was about this time I'd start crying uncontrollably. I go to sleep just so I don't have to sob into the late hours. Tonight, my mind was so consumed with seeing Charlie again, my eyes were merciful enough to spare me, and I went to bed dry.

I started working at dawn. This life came with a small farm, a few cows, pigs, and a chicken. It was my job to tend to them. The smell of the animal turds, coupled with the awe-inspiring sunrise, is evidence enough that this life is real. After feeding, cleaning, and killing the animals, my day was filled with picking berries and harvesting vegetables. Once finished, I felt the bar calling me. This time would be different though — I was a celibate with a date with destiny, simultaneously missing Charlie and hoping never to see him again.

Reluctant as I was, my memories refused to die without a fight. The whole walk, I was thinking of what I was going to say. I was so vulnerable, as fragile as glass. If they brought up the wrong thing, told me I was only deeper in someone else's reality, I would completely break down. If I could live through all of this without taking my life, I must really want to live. I just wish I could be left alone. That was the ultimate revelation of this experience. Isolation is life's greatest gift. For so long, I thought I needed Alexandra to be happy. It wasn't until I got her that I realized I was never more miserable. I am just a different breed, a product of the times. I don't even miss Hobbes.

When I finally arrived at the bar, the sun was creeping below the horizon. The usual cars were parked outside with the exception of a black van that had to be them. I was worried the locals were giving them hell, seeing as we don't take kindly to goth or any "liberal bullshit" around here. The closer I came to the door, the louder it became. The muffled sound of music that was unmistakably Alexandra-inspired. I couldn't help but think of her. I almost ran right back home, but just as I was about to turn around, the door burst open to an old cowboy storming out, and I saw TK, Sylvia, and Charlie playing at the end of the bar, all looking directly at me.

"You can't call this garbage music," the old cowboy spat, shaking his head as he left.

"It's not garbage, it's goth," I informed him and walked right in.

The music seemed to disturb and alienate everyone inside with the exception of one lonely, drunk hick trying to square dance all by himself to the gazed out dark waves. Sylvia was on keyboard and vocals, TK was on guitar, and Charlie was on electronic drums. This was the first time I saw a band live. Their hazy sound was like a mix of Molchat Doma and She Past Away, two of Alexandra's favorite international goth acts. I made my way to the bar as the eyes of my former fellows followed me. As hard as I screamed my order for a Bud, the bartender couldn't hear, nor could I understand her. She ended up passing me my usual Pabst, "on the house," I heard. When the song finally ended, they were showered with beer and boos.

"This is going to be our last song," TK informed the audience as they shouted for them to get off the stage.

"We'd like to dedicate it to an old friend in the audience," said Charlie before going into a drum intro.

I kept leaning up against the bar, drinking my beer and trying not to get too sentimental. The song wasn't my cup of tea, but neither was trying to rain on a musician's parade, so I stayed quiet while everyone else buried the band in their displeasures. When the band finally finished and they stepped off the stage, they were heckled half to death by these bunch of hicks. That didn't seem to deter them from walking right up to me and trying to blend back into the crowd though.

"We were hoping you'd be here," Charlie began.

"I only made it in time for the last song."

"We don't care what you missed. We need to talk to you."

"I left Los Angeles and never want to go back."

"Don't pretend coming here was a choice. In fact, you chose the very opposite of this and only wound up here because Master was merciful enough not to condemn you to limbo."

"I'm not even going to ask how you know all that, I'm just going to assume you know absolutely everything I do."

"Don't insult us. We know much more."

"Just tell me why you came here."

"I know you don't want to hear this, but we need your help."

"No thanks. I don't care if Alexandra dies in her simulation, I'm only looking out for me now."

"That's sad to hear you don't care about her anymore."

"You should be happy I decided to move on. I love it here. No one bothers me."

"You weren't happy being a part of our movement? Fighting for something greater than yourself?"

"No … but I'm curious … why do you need me?"

"Sounds like you want to come with us," Sylvia butt in.

"We're gathering the movement to make one last stand to rescue her. No one knows the federal building better than you do."

"If you can hack my mind, you can know just as much as I do."

"Yes, but you're the only person that has ever been on Master's floor. That means he thinks you're special. He won't hurt you. If you're with us, we can get to him and stop him."

"Stop Master? What will that do?"

"It will end every simulation. The fake world will fall. We will live true lives."

"For better or for worse?"

"For better."

"If all that's in it for me is getting to live a so-called real life, then I'm out. I can't tell the difference anymore, nor do I care."

"They have Hobbes."

"Who does?"

"The government abducted him from your apartment after you left. Don't you want to save him?"

I thought for a long second. "A little."

"A little? Some friend you are."

Just then, the front door of the bar was kicked open, and in came three outlaws, hiding their faces under black cowboy hats. One of them raised a pistol up into the air and fired off a few warning shots.

"Everybody, get out!" he shouted as all the patrons emptied out of the bar.

When I stepped away from the bar to get going, the outlaw pointed his gun at me and lifted his hat to reveal his true identity as a goon.

"Except you four. You stay right there," the goon commanded.

Once everyone was gone and the coast was clear, the goon fired his gun at me. Selflessly, TK stepped in front of the bullet and took the shot in his chest. It sent him flying back for me to catch. At first, his agonizing groans made me think he was a goner, but when I looked closer and pulled down his collar, I saw the bullet lodged in his bulletproof vest.

"You knew they were coming?"

"We were trying to get to you before they did," he groaned.

"You saved my life."

"You're damn right I did, now will you help us?"

Just as he asked, another shot flew right over our heads and blew up a few glass bottles decorating the wall behind the bar.

"We gotta run," said Charlie.

"No, we stay and fight," said Sylvia, surprisingly.

"Are you guys armed?" I asked Sylvia, who quickly pulled out a handgun of her own, TK too.

Charlie pulled me behind the bar as the other bodies in the room shot at each other in a classic O.K. Corral shootout. Glass and alcohol rained down upon us as the shots missed our comrades and shattered the well drinks on the wall. First one goon went down — Sylvia shot him in the head. Then another — TK landed a shot in each peck, making him drop his weapon, then his body. With one goon to two anarchists left, the last goon standing raised his arms in the air to surrender.

"We're not going to let you go," TK informed the goon.

"I am one of many." He smirked.

His smile triggered a tick when the corners of his lips hooked and pulled a pin inside his skull. As soon as he heard that tick, TK's eye split open and he threw Sylvia over the bar with him to take cover with Charlie and me.

"Get down!" shouted TK as a massive blast erupted out of the goon, sending a wall of fire above our heads that nearly took the damn roof off. Once the explosion settled, TK led the four of us out from behind the bar and through the black smoke and burning corral remains. We saw the exploded goon's flaming boots still standing. Seeing his innards, we learned he was somewhere between flesh and robot. Copper blood and adamantium bone. They always did feel cold manhandling me. We made our way outside and into the van. TK got behind the wheel, and we blazed down the highway as if my choice to join them was already made.

"If there is anything you need from your home, now's the time to say something," Sylvia stated.

"I'm good," I said.

"Fuck," Charlie blurted out.

"What?" everyone asked.

"Our instruments ... they're all gone," Charlie answered.

TK shook his head and shrugged. "They're only machines," he answered, looking forward, his one-track mind on the road.

We hit a long span of country I had never seen before this trip. Most of America was like this, room for everyone to flourish gone wasted. They wanted humans to concentrate and die. Wherever there were wide open spaces, there was the dream of freedom to be bored and useless. TK was constantly checking the rearview mirror, looking for any goons or cops on our tail, but they never came. The government must've wanted us back in Los Angeles. Keep your friends close and your enemies closer, the government thought. I came to this conclusion when at one point we ran out of gas, and TK only had ten dollars to his name, only to find the closest station was cheap enough at thirty cents a gallon to fill up our tank.

Once we got our gas, Sylvia and TK swapped places for TK to sleep in the passenger seat. When Charlie and I were left alone in the back of the van, the two of us had the heart-to-heart I dreaded.

"Was love all you thought it would be?"

"It wasn't even worth mentioning."

"Why? You wanted it for so long, you must've learned something."

"You won't get me to open up. Not to you. Not about this. All I have to say is don't get your hopes up, kid."

"They already are. Master said it himself — there's nothing more real than the love between Alexandra and me. We're meant to be."

"What does he know? Did he foresee me destroying his simulation?"

"No, but only because he didn't expect our intervention."

"You intervened? How? The spider?"

Charlie simply nodded. "I'm sorry if it hurt."

"Why wouldn't you let me be happy? You could've still had her. She and I were in a different world."

"If I didn't kill you, you would've — "

"Made love to your woman?" I interrupted.

"I couldn't let you do that," he leveled with me.

"I thought you said she wasn't *YOUR* woman."

Charlie just shrugged. He had nothing to say to that. I could feel the hatred bubbling up inside. I couldn't fight it. Not this time. I learned to stop suppressing my feelings. I could destroy this world too. He was asking for it.

"You little twat," my words escaped out of the tiny gaps between my gritting teeth.

I wrapped my hands around his neck in a desperate choke, pressing him up against the back of TK's seat so hard, it's a miracle he didn't wake up. My fingers sunk into his flesh, constricting his windpipe. If I kept this up any longer, lover boy would die in my hands. All his mother did to save him was slam her foot on the brake and send my head smashing into the back of TK's seat, this time waking him up.

"What the hell was that for?" TK asked Sylvia after being snapped awake.

"Don't you dare touch my baby," Sylvia screeched before putting the car into park and getting out of her seat to get on top of me and slap my half-dead, concussed face around a couple times. After laying in a few shots, Charlie grabbed his mother and stopped her from hurting me anymore.

"Stop, stop. It's okay. You can't blame him. I would've done the same."

Sylvia looked her son in the eye then checked out his neck, seeing fresh finger marks on either side.

"You bastard, I ought to kill you," she said to me.

"Ugh ...," I moaned in response.

She got up and spat in my face before getting back behind the wheel.

"You're lucky my son thinks we need you because I don't. I've always thought you were in our way."

The car ride was silent, though we all had a world of words we wanted to say.

"You know I read all your poems and looked at everything in your heart and mind," I broke the silence after an hour.

"That's why I gave it to you."

"If you want her, go get her, Charlie. I won't stop you."

Those words were able to mend whatever parts of our bond I had broken. Just a simple nod between us spoke volumes.

Once we passed through California's state limits, the police-presence quickly dawned on us. The van slowed down as we approached a checkpoint where an armed guard waited inside a booth. We stopped at the booth, and the guard approached Sylvia at the window. His Mind Tap read hers, and with a quick connect to her retina, he was able to see her government credentials and let her through. All drive long, helicopters flew above us, shinning spotlights down upon the landscape, tracing all. This had its upside; the night was so dark if you looked around, your eyes would start forming certain denizens out of the darkness that followed you until the helicopters shone light on them to make them disappear. The border between California and Arizona was nowhere near as locked down as the border into Los Angeles. The city's checkpoint required Charlie to hide in a secret compartment in the van while Sylvia, TK, and I were forced to have our Mind Taps recalibrated and our bodies patted down. Once we cleared the first two tests, the final test was for each of us to be interrogated.

"Where are you coming from?"

"Texas," we all answered.

"Reason for your trip?"

"Government business."

Our stories checked out, and we were able to get back on the road downtown where we parked the van in front of the very warehouse where I first met Charlie. We took the capsule down to the complete darkness of the basement. Once we stepped out of the capsule, the lights were switched on, and hundreds of anarchists were there to surprise us.

"Welcome back!" the anarchists all shouted at me, throwing black confetti, and adorning me with black leis.

"Are you talking to me?" I asked.

"Yes, of course," one comrade answered.

"We missed you," another elaborated.

Instead of going right to sleep, like I wanted to, my entire night became a party involving hundreds of anarchists to befriend. As any good cult ought to do, they embraced me with a showering of love that lasted hours, enough to fill any emotional void. All my feelings of unrequited love were forgotten and replaced by the movement's warm commitment. I signed up to their program from the bottom of my soul to the top of my mind. There was champagne spraying, beer chugging, food fights, dancing, a band playing anarchist anthems we all knew the lyrics to. We sang all night, filling the basement with a chorus of voices that echoed through every chamber of our skulls. Charlie, TK, and Sylvia spent my party watching how I assimilated into the group like I was their experiment. The music simply wouldn't stop, the party ended when the last anarchist finally passed out. After hours of our dead, drunken sleep, we were woken up by Charlie, TK, and Sylvia, who came around splashing rose water in our faces. Once we were all awake, they stood at the front of the room to call us to attention.

"Is everybody up?"

"Yes," the collective answered.

"Good. I hope you feel welcome now, Ovid."

"I do."

"Now that you see we don't mean to cause you any harm, we can start talking about how we can use you as our weapon to revolt against the government and break Alexandra out of her prison. This will obviously be a very dangerous, potentially deadly operation. We thank you for your help."

I wondered if running was still an option at this point, then finally surrendered to the movement's request. All this time, I was looking for a purpose, and whether I liked it or not, this was going to be it. My life would not be wasted.

"I'm in. Whatever you need me to do, I'll do it. You need me to take a bullet, I will."

"Thanks. TK, take it away from here." Charlie nodded at him.

"Tomorrow, we are going to storm the federal building. We'll have a heavy outpour of men attack the front then a smaller squad gather at the rear. As we challenge their exterior defenses, we will instruct our people on the inside to get our captains in the building. We will have to take the stairs first to the lobby, where Sylvia here will blow the door to let you all in, then up to Alexandra's floor, most likely having to fight our way up every story. Any government employees you see, you have to kill. No exceptions. It doesn't matter what you find them doing, you should have no sympathy. That's how the banality of evil works — the people cleaning the toilets are just as guilty as the people dropping the bombs. Once we reach the laboratory floor, we will free every specimen until arriving at lab seven, where Alexandra is held prisoner. Charlie then penetrates her simulation to rescue her while we take care of Doctor Yorgos. Once she's with us, we get her out of the building into safety."

"Any questions?" Sylvia asked.

Everyone seemed totally tapped into TK's vision and collectively answered "No," while I was still trying to wrap my head around the magnitude of it all.

"Excellent, now that we're all on the same page, take the rest of the day to prepare yourself mentally and physically. If you have family, tell them you love them."

"Now, everybody out; we want to be alone with Ovid."

All my new friends slowly got up, wished me well, and took off till TK, Charlie, Sylvia, and I were left to enjoy the trashed scene.

"Do you have a family?" Sylvia asked me.

"No," I answered.

"Are they dead?"

"Never born."

She shrugged, not caring to learn the rest.

"What would you like to do on your last day alive?" Charlie asked.

"I don't really care. I've already died and come back. There's nothing or no one I'm going to miss."

"You're a virgin, correct?"

I could feel my face blushing. All my life I was told it was nothing to be ashamed of, but here, I was so totally embarrassed.

"So, what if I am?" I asked.

"If you'd like to make love to someone, I can arrange that for you."

"I don't want to do anything that feels forced."

"It won't. I know at least one person that wants you."

"At least one?"

Charlie looked up, passed me, and smiled. I turned around and saw Mary and Lisa arriving out of the capsule and walking over to us. They were both dressed in skin-tight leather cat suits and black stilettos.

"I figured you'd be interested and called ahead. They both find you terribly attractive. We've talked about this."

"You want me to make love to them?"

"If that's what you want ... they want to make love to *you* ..."

I nodded gleefully, already feeling anxious. Mary and Lisa walked over.

"Welcome back, sorry we missed your party," lamented Mary.

"Yeah, we really wanted to come, but we got caught up at home," Lisa continued.

"You two are roommates?" I asked.

"*Sure ... roommates.*" Lisa laughed, passing seductive eyes to her mate.

"Ovid, can you fill Mary and Lisa in on the plan in private?" Charlie asked.

"Umm, I think I remember everything."

"Good. We'll give you three some privacy," said Charlie as he, TK, and Sylvia took the capsule up and out.

I had trouble looking them in the eye and keeping my head up, but with a single finger raising my chin, Mary was able to command my libido into her portal eyes.

"We know what we have to do," Mary said, lowering her voice an octave to a slower, "only you" sounding tone.

"That's right, ever since we first called you into our dungeon to interrogate you, we knew you were the perfect slave," Lisa said without hesitating to kiss me.

As her lips left mine, she bit a tiny piece of tissue to tug back in her grin, and while my lip was between her teeth, I blurted out, "*Slave?*"

"Pretend you're on the job. We're still your supervisors. You're going to do exactly as we say."

"Do you understand, slave?"

"Yes."

"Yes, Mistresses Mary and Lisa," they commanded.

"Yes, Mistresses Mary and Lisa," I repeated.

"Excellent, now strip."

I followed my orders perfectly. Once my clothes were off and I was as naked as the day I was born, Mistress Mary put a collar around my neck while Mistress Lisa attached the leash, and together they walked me around the room, taking off their clothes until the three of us were a dog pack. We humped all day and night.

Death, the Most Goth

Even though we dress funeral-ready, goths rarely get asked what they think happens after death. I suppose our aesthetics and symbols give off the impression we are either pagan, atheist, or Satanist, but this couldn't be further from the truth. Goths are as diverse as any scene. There are many shades of black. That said, even as a psychic, I can't comprehend what's beyond this plane of reality. However, if all this time alone has given me anything, it is the ability to imagine all sorts of fantastical possibilities.

Like a simulation, reality dissolves upon death but the person remains, or rather, their "personhood" remains. Not in their flesh, but in their spirit. Your flesh is fake. My white skin, my black clothes, all that was ever real was my soul, mind, and the music. I wonder if my mind will carry on with my soul, if I'll get to keep my memories after there's no use for them. I'm okay with losing them. You have to learn how to let go. That's the most goth thing anyone can do. To live the fullest life without material attachments, ready to die any day. The fullest emotions, the most concentrated tears and embraces, loves, and sorrows come only when you're prepared to die and live in the moment.

Death rock is a genre that could've only come out of Los Angeles. One-part punk, another part goth, bands like Christian Death make the night exciting and poetic. There is also 45 Grave, Alien Sex Fiend, and England's Rudimentary Peni. These are artists with real emotional issues. Fractured minds making fractured music that romanticize death as something seductive. This is music that makes little sense while the sun is out. Sunlight will retreat to these songs until shadows overpower the streets and suddenly, you look up and discover everlasting night. With fellow death rockers creeping up and down Sunset Boulevard, there is nothing left in life to fear. They reject life itself, that there is any inherent good in it. This rebellious rush in the air is captured in the sound.

The best death rockers make themselves superior to bands that only wax poetic about death and violence by living up to their poetry and committing violence, even suicide, like Rozz Williams. Bands like Kettle Kadaver, who's lead singer mutilated himself in front of live audiences in unprecedented ways, could've only played death rock. Not metal, not punk, not goth — those are all for posers. They would present themselves on a poster covered in blood, but did they ever know the feeling of bleeding so profusely?

I'm spinning death rock vinyl all night because this is the last blog post I will ever write. I might not live to see Sunday, but whatever happens, I'll finally be free. I prefer being a soul without a body to living in this simulation, but I would settle for complete non-existence. The first album I put on is of course, *Only Theatre of Pain*. Opening with "Cavity — First Communion," church bells ring through my room and usher in the skeletal drumming of George Belanger and serrated guitars of Rikk Agnew. Rozz's vocal starts softly then assaults the listener like a spellcaster as the song revs up. "Spiritual Cramp" shows Rozz's lyrics shine and transgress through every religious boundary. Then there's "Romeo's Distress," the band's anthemic goth elegy, bringing out every drop of darkness from Rozz's poetic, alien heart. Rozz obsessed over the right French transgressive poets that any true goth or punk ought to know — Baudelaire, Rimbaud, and Lautreamont.

All the goth I've ever absorbed in my life has prepared me for tomorrow. All the black I've worn, sleeping in coffins, dagger dances, eyeliner hieroglyphs, it's all made me so audacious.

CHAPTER ELEVEN

I woke up between my lovers a completely new person after losing my virginity. All my negative brain waves were recharged positive, making my body operate on a higher frequency. It's a shame it took me this long and only happened the day before I might have to sacrifice myself, but if such a cruel thing could happen to me, it only reinforced the idea I was living in reality.

I didn't want to wake up Mary or Lisa, so I stayed frozen in place. I just smiled from ear to ear in the dark. The sound of my smile pulling the skin of my face seemed to be enough to wake them though, because they both spun around, over to me. Mary began pulling my chest hairs with her fingers while Lisa lodged her leg between my thighs.

"Do you want to go again?" I asked.

"I'm afraid we can't. We have to get ready for work. Big day." Lisa winked.

"Yeah, thanks for waking us up so early." Mary gave me a peck on the neck.

"Was I a decent lover?" I asked.

"You were sweet and tender."

"And not one bit selfish. You were giving."

"That's good."

"If we can't make love again, can we at least make out?"

"No," Mary said before kissing me one last time and getting out of bed.

Lisa then did the same as they both began getting dressed.

"This was special."

"If I survive, we should do it again," I suggested.

Mary and Lisa just shrugged, passing smiles between each other.

"I love you, Ovid," said Mary.

"I also love you," followed Lisa.

"Really?"

"Sometimes it might seem like we're bullying you, but the same way you fell in love with Alexandra after watching her for two years, Lisa and I fell in love with you."

"We saw the kindness in your actions. We knew the sweetness of your thoughts. Having worked for the government as long as we have, we know how rare hearts like yours are. Everyone with any kind of power is just so shallow."

They finished getting dressed, kissed me on my forehead, then wished me goodbye before holding hands and walking to the capsule that launched them out. I realized then that I should've told them I loved them too instead of just harboring their love and not giving anything in return. I figured the only chance I'd get to do that again is if and when I saw them inside the federal building. I was too prone to hiding my feelings. Feelings hidden don't get recorded as feelings at all. I went to sleep to dream away the regret.

***

"Wake the fuck up!" shouted Charlie.

I snapped awake and saw him, TK, Sylvia, and an army of anarchists standing around my bed. They crept up on me like a band of ninjas.

"How are you guys so sneaky?" I groggily muttered.

"Get dressed. We're waiting on you."

"Give me a minute."

The army of anarchist waited in place while I washed and got ready. I returned to them dressed in black and joined them all in their ascent to the surface where together we would storm the government gates, the federal front.

We piled out of the capsule in groups, our gang growing on the street like gangrene until flooding it from sidewalk to sidewalk, attacking the block. Our cloud of black began marching, and before we knew it, cyber cops were already stationed in wait. Shots were fired between both sides, and one of theirs died for every two of ours. Our sea of bodies overwhelmed their small numbers, and we kept pushing forward toward the evil tower. Whatever forces the government sent to fight us off before we arrived at their door were quickly steamrolled. They couldn't hold a candle against the winds of revolution. When we finally turned down the street that would lead us directly to the federal building's front doors, the long walk of our anarchist army turned into a tidal wave, running on the war cries of our spirited brethren. We hit the front and flanked the back, our second army arriving only moments after our first. The building was surrounded, and where other efforts looked like a protest, this was unmistakably war. Our anarchist guitarist plugged in and began playing the head-splitting, wall of noise notes that would neutralize their Mind Tap network. Unlike before, the federal building's exterior weaponized itself, revealing turrets out of the base that shot and killed men and women on our front line. Those that died went in willingly, martyrs for their children's sake. They had to stay put, wait, and die until we were inside. I stood back with TK, Sylvia, and Charlie until we stopped at a manhole. We waited there, watching the havoc being waged upon our friends, trying not to break down crying. Gang morale was high, subverting our sadness. Suddenly, the manhole began to slowly spin open until it lifted off the street revealing Hobbes, coming to our rescue.

"Took you long enough." TK shook his head and started descending down the manhole.

"Good job, Hobbes," Charlie said, disregarding TK's displeasure.

I wasn't sure whether I was angry at Hobbes or relieved to see him.

"When this is all said and done, we need to have a chat," I said.

He simply nodded and waddled down the street, away from the action and hopefully home. The three of us headed underground, into the sewer system that ran underneath the federal building. It was murky and wet down there. Our boots were covered in what had to be shit. TK pulled out a flashlight and led the way until we arrived at a steel door at the side of the tunnel.

"Mary and Lisa should be waiting on the other side."

TK began tapping his flashlight against the door in coded rhythm to ensure Mary and Lisa it was us. We heard the door unlocking from the other side until it flew open, revealing behind it three smiling goons with guns. The first goon's gun was pointed directly at TK's head. Even with a gun between his eyes, we couldn't help but drift our sights to the goon's feet, where Mary and Lisa's dead bodies lay. A single tear would've gotten him killed, but I was lucky enough to have the luxury to shed a few. Instead, TK reflexively grabbed the goon's wrist and twisted it, turning his smile upside down and sending his gun into his chest to fire three rounds.

He wished a few of those bullets shot out the other side to kill the other goons, but he wasn't so lucky. The first goon fell, and the next drew his weapon only to get shot in the head by Sylvia. By the time my gaze bounced from Sylvia's target back to her, the gun was already smoking, the goon already dead. The last goon's last resort was to self-destruct, but before he could, TK slammed the door in his face. The explosion blew the hinges off the door, making its warped frame fall to the ground before our feet. After that, the scene was clear for our entry. We were forced to walk over the charred remains of Mary, Lisa, and the goons. I couldn't help but cry; I wasn't built for war. I should've been thinking about dodging and firing bullets, but instead my mind was occupied by regret. Never miss an opportunity to tell someone you love them. As I wiped my eyes, Charlie turned to me to get my head back in the game.

"Save your tears for when we set Alexandra free."

"They were the only people that ever loved me," I bemoaned.

"You don't even know the half of it. They weren't trying to grant you your last wish — making love to you was fulfilling theirs. They were head over heels in love with you. They knew this was a suicide mission."

I slurped up all the snot coming out of my nose and wiped my tears dry. We ran down an underground tunnel to a dead end with a torch hung upon the wall. TK pulled that torch to trigger a false wall to open and reveal our way forward. We found ourselves in the dungeon and ran for a door that led to the stairs. We ran our way up to the lobby, three flights of stairs above us. Once we made our way up, we opened the door to the lobby and saw all our forces on the other side of the building's windows. The floor was packed with goons wielding automatic rifles, waiting for us to show our faces.

"Never forget Mama loves you. Now go get your goth girl," Sylvia told Charlie.

"I love you too, Mom," he replied.

Sylvia dove through the door in matriarchal martyrdom to let our forces in to flood the building. She ran, tumbled, rolled, and jumped over and under a foray of bullets that only ended up generating goon casualties. When she finally made her way to the front door, she planted a bomb and quickly detonated it right there, killing herself but letting the anarchists in. The last thing we saw before we kept running up the stairs was the explosion enveloping Sylvia. Even still, Charlie didn't make so much as a whimper.

Within the time it took to climb three flights of stairs up to the third floor, our anarchists started spilling into the stairwell after taking the lobby. With every story they climbed, a group of anarchists would leave the stairwell to attack each floor in our attempt to conquer the building from bottom to top. The orders given to our anarchists were simple: kill anyone that isn't your own. Whether the government employees were brewing coffee or organizing death camp records, they would have to go. After a while, from out of each floor, goons would enter the stairwell to meet us. Our gang of three retreated and let our minions assume the front lines to fight them off. Soon, the entire stairwell was consumed with ultra-violence. Bullets flying and bouncing about, killing goons and friends that weren't even aimed at. Bones were cracked and organs burst by goons and anarchists in hand-to-hand combat. Back and forth, some of theirs and some of ours were thrown down the stairwell to fall multiple stories to their deaths.

When we reached the tenth floor, where I worked, the door flung open to a giant goon, twice the size of the average. He was some sort of mutant, a laboratory creation. His muscles nearly tore through his skin, and you could see his veins protrude through his clothes as they ran up his arms, chest, neck, and face. He was what you'd call a berserker. When our anarchists attempted to shoot him, the bullets had their skulls caved in against his body before meaninglessly falling to the ground.

"It's doctor's orders I kill you all," the goon muttered.

He grabbed the first anarchist in his way by both arms and tore them clean out of their sockets then used them to bash more anarchists across the face. Men were bludgeoned, killed, and eviscerated in waves as we kept pushing and crashing against the goon. It was complete carnage. None of us expected to meet such an immovable object, so there was no plan in place to defeat him. Certainly, we couldn't match his force. Luckily for us, TK thought of solutions quickly and deduced the best way to neutralize the giant was using an enemy resource and flipping it against them. TK walked back through the ranks of our army a few stories down to meet the anarchist guitar player who was hard at work wailing on his guitar to keep the Mind Tap network down. In a move of pure genius, TK silenced him so the network could be restored. Now that his Mind Tap was on, TK simply lifted the giant goon off his feet and floated him up to the very top of the building.

"When I say now, you play guitar," he instructed the guitarist.

Now that the giant floated fancifully through the air like a balloon, he took on a rather goofy appearance.

"You bastard, as soon as I get down from here, I'll snap your body in half," the goon benignly growled.

He threatened to break every bone and burst every organ in our bodies before finally reaching the ceiling, and once he did, with his back, arms, and legs pressed flat against it, TK knew it was time to give our guitarist his cue.

"Now!" TK shouted, making the guitarist strum his weapon with deafening volume.

The sound dropped the network again, cutting the telekinetic connection between TK's Mind Tap and the goon. As swiftly as a hanged man drops when his noose is snapped with a blade, the goon fell thirty-five stories, tumbling down the stairwell, bashing his face in along the way. The impact of his fall was so strong, when he hit the bottom, the splat sent his guts and gears flying back up to us.

We kept moving forward and upward, dripping sweat through our black clothes on the climb. It was the same pattern on every floor, killing goons and storming stories until the building was purged of government scum. It wasn't until we reached the twentieth floor that we decided to pause and let the boys take a moment to rest. This small breath between battles saw little debate or deliberation as to what steps to take next or what to anticipate. We were too concerned with healing to think. In the relative silence of this moment, we barely noticed the next mini-boss sashay into our midst. This one was a perfect replica of Alexandra that strode into the stairwell with sultry eyes that landed upon Charlie and me.

"Where do you boys think you're going?" she asked.

The entire army of anarchists came to a dead halt behind TK, Charlie, and I as we tried to understand what sort of demon stood before us.

"She's a trap," I warned.

"A trap? How could you say that? I thought you were here to rescue me," she said, a bit offended.

"Shut up, you duplicate bitch," I snapped back at her.

"Wait, don't be so quick to judge. We should listen to her," Charlie reasoned, staring at her, almost hypnotized.

TK looked into Charlie's eyes and saw the delusion in them. He gave him a stiff slap to the back of the head to snap him out of it.

"Gah, what was that for?" Charlie said, rubbing out the ache.

"Get your head out of your ass before you get us killed."

"Why don't you give me a kiss, Charlie? You'll see I'm the real deal." Alexandra winked at him as she puckered her lips.

"I'm going to shoot," TK said as he raised his high-power hand cannon and pointed it directly into Alexandra's porcelain face.

"Wait," Charlie said, trying to pull TK's arm down.

"For what?"

"They're expecting us to attack."

"You think she's a Trojan horse?"

"I do. The best thing we could do is avoid her completely. Anything might trigger some kind of reaction. A kiss or a bullet."

Charlie merely tiptoed past her, waving at us to follow.

"If Charlie won't kiss me, maybe you will, Ovid. You've always deserved me more anyway."

"Sorry, babe, but I'm holding out for something real."

I quickly slithered past her and went after Charlie, trying not to look her in the eye.

"What's the matter, boys? Don't you love me anymore?"

"You're not Alexandra. You're a machine," TK said to her.

"Who are you again? Oh, the programmer — how sad." Alexandra scrunched her lips to one side before turning to us. "Don't listen to him. He's just jealous. I can prove I'm Alexandra."

"Please don't," Charlie begged.

"You're my little white butterfly," Alexandra told Charlie, only now in Sylvia's voice.

Charlie's heart sank as the voice activated primal feelings of sadness and rage.

"Shut up," he snarled, appearing to cry for the first time in front of me.

"Butterflies may appear beautiful, but they're actually rather cruel, drinking the blood of other beings. A butterfly never knows its mother, it survives without affection, and grows cold and vampiric. Just like us. We're so cold there's no blood running through our veins," Alexandra continued, still in the same voice and cadence as Charlie's martyred mother.

"I knew my mother. She was beautiful. She raised a good person. Too good not to catch a fake," Charlie spat quiet venom at her through his tears.

"That's it, I've had enough." TK locked and loaded his gun, ready to blow Alexandra's head off.

She turned back to TK and stepped into his gun.

"I suggest you pull the trigger. Shooting me will make this bitter moment sweet."

"Run!" Charlie shouted as he and I sprinted up the stairs away from our brothers.

Alexandra stepped forward and softly kissed TK's lips. The moment she did, her body exploded into an inferno that covered every floor beneath Charlie and I in flames. Though the black smoke blinded us from seeing anything behind us, Charlie and I had no doubt TK was dead. There was no more anarchist army now. It was only Charlie, me, silence, and fire. We had little time if we wanted to reach the laboratory before suffocating, so we ran harder and faster than any point in our lives. On my way up, my boot stepped over TK's blown off, cleft lip. By the time Charlie and I reached the top, we may have appeared unscathed, but we were heartless.

The last door in the stairwell took us to the laboratory. Without TK or any backup, we wouldn't have enough muscle to put up a fight against any number of enemies. We had to be sneaky, we thought. The moment we entered the laboratory floor though, we realized all the hallways were deserted. Expecting an ambush, we slowly stalked our way through, treading lightly and scanning every direction for a threat.

"Are we going to rescue the other experiments?" I asked.

"No," Charlie lamented. "We'll be lucky just to get to Alexandra."

My concern didn't matter though; every lab appeared to be empty and barren, as if no foul play ever took place beyond the glass separating us. When we finally arrived at laboratory seven, the door was already open and waiting for our arrival. We stepped through the door, and there was Doctor Yorgos, standing in front of dozens of different sharp medical instruments, all spread out on a metal table. Above Yorgos were two television screens, one showing us Alexandra inside her simulation in her house, the other outside her simulation in her cube. She was lying in bed, quietly reading. To Yorgos's left was Alexandra's simulation space, where all that separated us from her was a giant gallery window.

"My life's work, all gone to hell because of your misguided meddling. Whether you two survive your surgeries or not, there's no going back for me or Alexandra. The experiment can no longer continue. In other words, I have nothing to lose. My life is meaningless without my work."

"Your work was reprehensible. Torturing and exploiting a child to inspire technology? You disgust me," Charlie began.

"I don't expect you to understand why Alexandra's happiness and wellbeing was worth sacrificing for our vision of the future. Just know the world is a better place because of my work and her 'torturing' as you put it," Yorgos replied.

"I wouldn't get so hung up on your great contributions to science, Doctor. Your name will be forgotten after today," I interjected.

"That's right. I hope we don't find the same joy in making people suffer as you, but we're about to find out," said Charlie.

"Really, Ovid? Is that really what you think? I always thought you were an admirer of mine."

"I've considered you scum since day one."

"The programming I installed in you must've never been properly activated then. You remember that one time you were foolish enough to volunteer going under my knife, don't you? Perhaps I'll try rebooting that program now."

Doctor Yorgos pulled one of his hands out of his lab coat and snapped his fingers, flipping a switch in my brain. I could sense a part of me fading away. Order must be upheld. Charlie is chaos — the chaos that resides within all humanity. Chaos must not be allowed to proliferate. Charlie must not leave this place alive. Anarchy must be thwarted. Order will be restored when he dies.

"Do you still think I'm such a bad man?"

"You altered the path of humanity that we may one day become Gods. You're a genius."

"That's right. *See*, you understand me … but Charlie, the only one of us to never have a Mind Tap, thinks he has something in common with my specimen. How can you ever know what it's like to be a God like us?"

"Who gives a shit about Gods? What do you know about being human? A lowlife like you is an insult to our entire species. We will all be better off once you're gone."

"Then go ahead, get rid of me, but I warn you, I leave a stain."

Charlie quickly grabbed one of the medical utensils on the table. I grabbed his wrist to stop him before he could stab the good doctor, but as it would turn out, Yorgos was not his target. With one hand in my grip, Charlie used his other to grab another scalpel and drive it directly into my temple, stabbing my Mind Tap. A shock ran through my body, and I folded up like an accordion. My hand around his wrist went limp as I collapsed to the ground. All I could move was my eyes, which saw my blood spilling out of my head to pool around Charlie's boots.

"Look what you did," Doctor Yorgos scolded Charlie. "You said you wanted to kill me. Not Ovid."

"I didn't kill him. I had to get rid of his Mind Tap. He's fine. He just needs a second, you'll see. Right Ovid?" Charlie asked, tears escaping his eyes from the intensity.

"These people were never your friends," Doctor Yorgos told me, shaking his head.

"Don't listen to him. I am your friend. Now I need you to get up and help me fight."

Their words sounded muffled, like I was listening to them underwater. My mind was clear though. Without a Mind Tap, I felt no allegiance to either extremist. My commitment to the anarchist cause was a consequence of Charlie's hacking just as much as my obedience to Yorgos was a consequence of a government hack. My natural brain was all that was left, and it had no masters. I was not on either side. I was the line that separated them. I was the truth. I would not die, not now.

Not without embracing Alexandra for real. With this affirmation, an electrical current returned to my hands, and I was able to pull my face off the floor. From my hands to my arms, half my body returned to me. From my body to my legs, I stood up tall before Charlie and Doctor Yorgos, newly resurrected and deciding who to kill. I pulled the knife out of my head and, after thinking for a split second, sent it flying at the doctor's face. It stopped midair, a millimeter from his forehead, and turned around to face me.

"You overcame my programming. What a shame. No matter. Unlike your friend, I make my cuts count."

He sent the scalpel back at me, fast as a bullet, but again, it stopped, this time a molecule away from penetrating my eye. I dared not blink and sever the eyelid. I wondered who could've possibly rescued me. The only one with a Mind Tap among us was Yorgos.

"If neither of you stopped it, then who — "

Yorgos and I turned our attention to the gallery window, where Alexandra's mother, Vera, stood in total concentration as her Mind Tap kept the blade from harming me.

"What the hell are you doing out of the simulation? I'll have you strung to pieces for this," Yorgos seethed.

"I will not let you harm her anymore," said Vera, with fire in her eyes.

Charlie looked past Vera to the two-story white cube that sat beyond the glass. Alexandra was hanging out her window, admiring the white butterfly. The moment Charlie saw her, everything seemed to freeze except the layer of tears forming over his eyes. Suddenly, he didn't care about killing Yorgos — Vera and I would have to figure that out ourselves. He wanted to see Alexandra and wanted her to see him.

"Get down, now!" Charlie shouted at Vera.

Charlie then reached for the table, holding all Yorgos's utensils, and with unnatural strength, lifted and threw the entire piece of furniture through the gallery window, shattering it into hundreds of pieces. Vera dove out of the table's way, completely unharmed and with her concentration holding up the knife unbroken. Meanwhile, having never heard such a noise in her life, Alexandra turned in our direction. Still in her simulation, she could hear us but not see us.

"Alexandra!" Charlie shouted as he hopped over the broken window and into her experiment.

He ran past her mother to her white cube and called to her from below her window. The butterfly fluttered off, and now she was alone with Charlie's voice.

One screen above Doctor Yorgos showed Charlie standing at the foot of the white cube outside of the simulation. The other screen showed Alexandra in her house, looking down from her window upon nothing at all. Vera, Yorgos, and I lowered our defenses to witness this moment. The moment was stronger than our desire to kill each other. It was the moment a dream came true, and a love was born.

"Alexandra, are you okay?" Charlie asked.

"Who said that? Where are you?"

"It's Sylvia's son, Charlie. I exist outside of your simulation."

"Sylvia has a son?"

"Yes. I fought my way here to rescue you."

She had to think for a second, a little shocked the moment she was always waiting for had finally arrived. She still wasn't sure if Charlie was really the one.

"What's your favorite band?"

"The Cure."

Alexandra put one hand over her heart and smiled before saying, "I am ready to be rescued."

Like a gecko, Charlie scaled the side of the cube to her window and raised himself up to her. The only way someone on the outside could break inside the simulation was to interact with Alexandra, so he drew his face close to hers until she could taste his breath. She then opened her mouth to receive his, and they kissed for the first time, crumbling the fabric of the false world around her. Reality awoke from its slumber. As the simulation dissolved, the white cube appeared with Charlie before her. Alexandra's eyes were opened for the first time, and the first thing she saw was the goth of her dreams all dressed in black inside her white room.

"Let's get out of here," Charlie suggested.

Alexandra grabbed Chastity before Charlie hopped into her window and took her hand for them to run down the stairs and out of the cube.

The moment was too beautiful to understate, but as Vera and I let our guards down, Yorgos capitalized on our vulnerable pause by controlling the knife that was still suspended right in front of me to shoot into Vera's neck. The sound of the blade severing flesh and bone, coupled with the sound of blood spurting out of the hole were unforgettable. Gurgling through her quick death, the crudeness of her momentary agony before she simply dropped triggered the most animalistic blood-thirst in me.

"No!" I screamed as Yorgos laughed.

I hopped over the table and pounced on him before he had the chance to use his Mind Tap. Before he knew it, fist after fist connected with his face. There was no psychic force stopping me from bashing in his skull. Once not a piece of pulp was left of him, I ran over to Vera's side to find Alexandra and Charlie kneeling over her. The wound in her neck seemed to be missing and completely healed, the knife was still bloody but now resting at her side.

"It's no use. She's gone," Alexandra lamented with a tearful choke in her voice.

"I'm so sorry, Alexandra."

"How did this happen?" she asked, sobbing.

"She tried to stop Doctor Yorgos from hurting you."

I walked over to them and knelt down next to Alexandra to console her.

"Your mother saved my life."

"She wasn't my mother … but I loved her like one."

"The only way to honor her now is to escape with us. So, there's no time to cry," Charlie's lament was too serious to be sorrowful.

He helped Alexandra to her feet, and for the first time, she and I took a good look at each other. She then placed her palm over my bleeding temple.

"Come closer."

I leaned my wound into her hand, and like magic, she tethered together the fine tendrils of broken flesh until it was healed. I touched the spot and felt no pain then embraced her, tightly, because I was so happy that she was finally free. When I pulled away, she looked at me, and her eyes glistened as if she recognized me.

"Do I know you?" she asked.

"No, but I know you. I am Ovid, your Overseeing Voyeur. I watched you inside that cube for two years. I even read your book."

"Are you Sylvia's friend?"

"Yes. At least I was."

"Charlie?" she asked, confused and disappointed.

"Yes?"

"Where is Sylvia?"

"She's gone … just like your mom."

"Sylvia died?"

"Yes. Trying to rescue you."

"And you're not crying?"

"Because I know she would be so happy right now."

"I suppose that makes us orphans," Alexandra said and stepped forward as if leading our way out.

We left out the same door we entered and made our way down the empty laboratory floor. The stairwell was still on fire, but now with Alexandra, many new methods of escape were possible. Alexandra held Chastity close to her chest as she followed us over to an open capsule, and we entered then pressed the button for lobby. The capsule doors closed, and after descending only a single floor, we came to a dead halt.

"What's going on?" Charlie asked.

"Never seen this before."

"Something wrong?" Alexandra asked.

"Yes, we need to get out of the building. This was supposed to take us to the ground floor."

"Oh, you want to leave? Why didn't you say so? There are plenty of ways to do that."

Alexandra squinted, and we both just assumed she was ready to blow the roof sky high for us to escape until anti-climactically, nothing happened, and she stepped back, bothered.

"What's wrong?" Charlie asked.

"It didn't work," Alexandra groaned.

"What didn't work?" I asked.

"I tried to make a hole in the floor for us to float out of, but it wouldn't work," Alexandra lamented, shocked.

Suddenly, a movie began playing on the capsule's glass for us to watch. It began with an old-fashioned black-and-white countdown, and when it reached one, a black-and-white map of Africa appeared, meaning it could only be *Casablanca*.

"*Casablanca?*" Charlie asked.

"This wouldn't be the first time it's been shoved in my face — someone must be trying to tell me something," I disclosed.

We were treated to a strange cut of the film with scenes missing from the original. A barroom brawl, a long kiss between Bogie and Ingrid, Victor Laszlo's suicide from a bullet to the head. It was a manipulation and bastardization of the past. Sam played a tune on the piano while Humphrey Bogart stood over him, smiling over a glass of whiskey before sauntering over to us.

"Charlie, Ovid, Alexandra. You three have come a long way to get this far. Are you sure you know where you're going?"

"No," answered Alexandra, the one among us that knew the least about our intentions.

"You really don't know? That's a shame. Seems like you two clowns really got the poor girl spooked."

"We're just trying to go home," I told Bogie.

"You a part of this plot, doll?" Bogie asked her.

Alexandra pointed to herself, not sure who Bogie was addressing. He took a sip then nodded at her to confirm her suspicion. "I guess so," she answered.

"Then let me show you the way out."

The capsule's frame began to warp around us until its tunnel's vertical dimensions took on the horizontal dimensions necessary to pass through the building's center. From the building's edge, our vessel began crawling inward.

"Do you know why my powers won't work?"

"Can't say I do." Bogie shrugged.

The capsule arrived behind a wall that slid open to reveal the beginning of the spiral hallway on the thirty-fourth floor. The capsule doors opened to let us out, and we stepped forward into the hallway. The capsule then retreated back into the tunnel, and the wall slid closed to become the same dead-end I encountered upon my last visit here, only this time, instead of Little Richard's portrait, David Bowie's adorned the hallway's start, meaning the order of the portraits was reversed. Alexandra was in awe, overjoyed to see the portraits of all her punk heroes. We treaded down this stretch of Master's mind from Bowie to Iggy all the way to Little Richard, taking the spiral to its end at the center where we met the door to his office. I opened the door and saw everything in the office was the same except each star's position in the cosmic background. I didn't need to ask; I knew the room mimicked the Earth's rotation.

"Hello?" My words echoed into the void.

Master seemed to walk so lightly, he floated over to us from the shadows without casting one.

"If you came this far, then my kingdom has fallen. Ovid, this is the second creation of mine you've destroyed."

"Thank you for sparing my life the first time. I'm sorry I lost my cool."

"No need to apologize if you intend to do it again."

Master moved his glance to Alexandra. There was a sparkle in his eye as he admired her.

"How does it feel to finally be out of your fish tank?"

"Smells a little strange, but I like it so far."

Master considered her answer. "How do you wish it smelled?"

"Like lavender?" She shrugged.

With a blink, Master made everything smell purple.

"I'm impressed," Alexandra said.

"Are you?" Master asked.

"Yes … you're David Bowie, aren't you?" Alexandra asked.

"Why do you say that?" Master asked back.

"I recognize your face. Your eyes. I've been a fan of you all my life."

"I'm sorry, I can't say I am … Just for jollies, though, what's your favorite album?"

"I'm an eighties geek. I like *Let's Dance*."

"Oh, that one was written for you," he said before walking over to his throne and waving us over to join him. "Take a seat."

There were three empty seats waiting for us.

"So, what did you come here to ask me?" Master asked as he sat down.

"We just want to go home," Charlie begged.

"Did she try clicking her heels three times?" Master asked, pointing at Alexandra.

She looked down and clicked them three times. Nothing.

"Now what?" Alexandra asked.

"If you're still here, you must not have any powers."

"I've noticed. Why is that?" Alexandra asked.

Master reached into his pocket and pulled out a knife. Out of nowhere, he threw the knife directly at Alexandra, and she stopped it before it flew even an inch from his hand.

"Hey, my powers are back," she happily realized.

"For as long as I allow you to have them back," Master replied.

"So, you are able to control her?" I asked.

"What if after you left your simulation you entered a world where you never had powers in the first place but then crossed into a different world when you entered this room? What if each of you is in a different reality, and your powers don't work in one of them? And what if my only power is being able to control you, Alexandra? Two of these are true, can you guess which is false?"

"You control me?" Alexandra asked if he did.

"False," he answered that he did, in fact, control her.

"Your first proposition was false, and the two latter are true. One of us are not real, and you control Alexandra's powers. What about *Casablanca*? How'd you change the film?" I asked.

"What if I used Alexandra's powers to change *Casablanca*? What if Alexandra isn't only able to manipulate space, but she can also manipulate time and never knew it? What if I controlled Alexandra to make every second you live take place in a different reality with some of those seconds taking place in simulations? What if you spend your life with one foot in the real and another in the fabricated, only half alive? What if life is like a deck of cards, the black cards real, the red cards fake, and time is just a shuffled deck being played out for you? Two of these propositions are true," Master continued.

"Deck of cards?" Charlie asked, utterly confused.

"False," he answered, confusing us more.

"The first and second proposition are true. You used Alexandra's powers to go back in time and re-edit the film."

"This means she's been more powerful than she ever knew," Charlie added.

"I control time?" Alexandra asked, shocked.

"Yes, try making a hole in the wall and flying us out of here," I suggested as a test.

"She'll be doing nothing of the sort," Master said.

Alexandra squinted, attempting to use her mind to open a portal out of Master's office, but it was no use.

"I will let you go when I'm good and ready. Before that, I want to tell you the story of our special girl here."

"We're in no rush." Charlie nodded to Alexandra then Master, wanting to hear the story.

"I died in the year 2016. In those days, there was no way to preserve my body or mind. The best anyone could do was put my memories on a hard drive and my sperm inside a test tube. My memories were downloaded into an android in the year 2048. Now a machine-man, I financed an experiment that would manipulate my DNA to create a special child. One who's body I could one day take as my own. Most of the children that came from my seed were failures. Except you, Alexandra. You were never meant to be a weapon; you were meant to be a vessel. However, your powers were so great I didn't need to take your body. Instead, I could use your powers to resurrect my flesh. All the other experiments failed, but with you, they produced a success beyond my wildest dreams, able to manipulate time and space. In the brief span of time that you were aware of your true power, you folded time and pulled my body out of the past and into the present. You were thirteen years old when you did this."

"I don't remember every doing that."

"We installed a Mind Tap to control your powers then wiped your memory and made sure you forgot."

"How do you control me now?"

Master put his hand against Alexandra's temple.

"We never removed that Mind Tap. Unlike everyone else's though, I am the only one with access to it. That's why you had that dream."

"The man who fell to Earth," she muttered.

"You remember," Master glowed.

"I'd really like it if you gave up control," Alexandra said.

"You think you're ready for that kind of responsibility? That would make you the master of all this." Master gestured the entire room with his hands, meaning the entire universe.

"Yes."

"You are my daughter. I owe you my life. You have to pass a test and show me you're ready."

"What do we have to do?" Charlie asked.

"If you can leave this building, I will disable your Mind Tap and relinquish control."

"That doesn't sound too difficult. What's the catch?" I asked.

"No catch, just a clue — If you fail, you'll be seeing me again. If you succeed, then you won't."

Using Alexandra's mind, Master was able to create a wrinkle in the room that split the ground and opened to a set of stairs that resembled the same stairwell we climbed up the building. Master gestured for us to follow the stairs down, and the three of us began to walk. We walked and walked until we saw in the corner of the stairwell, Master sitting there, smoking and nodding at us as we passed by.

"If you see me, you know you failed. So, keep trying," Master spoke between drags.

We failed so fast we didn't even realize the test had begun. We kept walking down flights of stairs, counting all the while until we climbed down thirty-four stories. On the thirty-fifth, we saw him again, in the same corner, not a single centimeter of his cigarette burned since the last time we saw him.

"Try again," he said, then smoked, shaking his head.

"What are we doing wrong?" Charlie asked.

Master's lips were sealed, only opening to blow smoke in Charlie's face. This time, as we descended the stairs again, counting the stories, we sifted through everything Master said to isolate the clues and toss out the jargon.

"He's folding space, so whenever we reach the bottom, we arrive back at the top," Charlie figured.

"No, no, no, he's folding time, so the beginning is the end. That's why he's still on the same cigarette," I hit back.

"How do you know it's the same one?"

"I don't."

"Right. Then shut up," Charlie said, finally frustrated.

"Don't be rude. Ovid is trying to help," Alexandra shot him down.

"You're right. I'm sorry," he apologized.

"No problem. What else did Master say?"

"That we may be living with one foot in reality and another in a simulation."

"So, this could be another fake?"

"Does it even matter?"

"Can't tell."

"Then don't try," I said, finishing off an angry ping-pong between Charlie and I.

Chastity started hissing at us and slashed us both across our cheeks with her claws. Alexandra pulled Chastity back, making sure she couldn't take more of her frustrations out on our flesh.

"Stop, the both of you," Alexandra snapped at us.

"Sorry," we both apologized simultaneously.

"If he's controlling my mind to simulate an endless stairwell, why don't you just knock me unconscious. He can't control a mind that isn't awake," Alexandra genuinely suggested.

"We're not doing that," I replied.

"No way. Keep walking," Charlie seconded.

By the time we reached this tense deadlock, we had already passed thirty-five stories and came up on Master, still smoking that supposed same cig. The cuts Chastity had landed on our faces now disappeared, meaning time was being manipulated to create this puzzle.

"If we kill you, would this all stop?" Charlie asked.

"You can't kill me unless I want to die."

Charlie pulled out a gun he pointed directly at Master's face.

"You've been carrying a piece this entire time?" I asked.

"I don't like using it, but I don't think I have a choice anymore."

"Was it worth it?" Master asked in advanced.

Charlie fired, but the bullet lodged in the gun, exploding it in his hand. His flesh and bone mangled around the metal only long enough for him to scream. His screams echoed infinitely up and down the never-ending staircase. A moment later, the space around his hand divorced itself from all other space to let time rewind and reform the flesh as good as new, like nothing happened.

"Every little joy you three have ever known was a consequence of my decisions and mercy. You're very lucky to have a father like me, Alexandra."

"I know I am."

"Surely you take after me enough to figure out this little puzzle, don't you?"

She turned her face up to the stairs, and together, we decided to ascend the stairs instead of taking them down, realizing if we climbed up from the thirty-fifth floor, it wouldn't take us to the roof but right back to the bottom. And we were correct — we arrived at the bottom of more stairs that we walked up, another thirty-four floors just to arrive back at Master's side.

"Charlie considered force. Alexandra attempted reversal. What about you, Ovid? You were always the smartest, what do you suggest?"

"I wouldn't be an overseeing voyeur if I wasn't paying close attention to everything I've seen and heard up to this point. Not just now or in my time with you but throughout my entire life. What makes an experience real or fake can be deduced to certain perceptible details. The devil is in the details, and your fakery is hell. Yet, you are merciful enough to extend us a hand from time to time and give us lowly humans a hint to use as rope and pull ourselves out of the quicksand. No, Charlie, we cannot force our way out of this place. And no, Alexandra, in a world of falsity, the reversal is not reality but an opposite and equal falsity. Two things you mentioned really struck me, Master. First, the suggestion that it was possible that each of us can be experiencing different realities or simulations. So, if one of us was in a simulation and the other two were in reality, then together, all three would end up in that one's simulation. The second thing was something you said a long time ago, that there's nothing more real than the love between Charlie and Alexandra.

"You love me?" Alexandra asked Charlie.

Forced to come up with an answer, Charlie was unable to hide his feelings anymore. There was no use waiting, anything short of the truth in this moment would damn them all to an eternity of lies.

"With all my heart," Charlie answered.

She quickly lunged into his embrace, and the two began to make out as if Master and I were imaginary, potentially because we were.

"That would mean Alexandra and Charlie are real, here, together, in love."

"Then what would that make you, my dear overseeing voyeur?"

"It would make me fake, wouldn't it?"

"If you say so, but how could you know?"

"Oh, I know. Not just by process of elimination. No, there are qualities to the life I've been living, the life you gave me, that have always felt fake."

"Please, go on," Master wished.

"All my life, I've wanted one thing: to be loved. It only came to me the day before my lovers perished. I would've loved Mary and Lisa with all my heart and been loyal to them until the day I died. I swear this with all my real soul, wherever it may be. Such a cruel fate befell me for one simple reason: I am not living a real life. I've been living in a dream land of some kind, chasing ghosts and mirages.

They were all made up. Maybe I was made up too. Or maybe everything I was taught was a fake to simplify a reality too complex to be worth explaining. Those that live real lives, they find what they're looking for. This pain I've been subjected to, it's not the nature of reality to do that to anyone."

"You do know reality can be a more painful and twisted experience than any simulation, don't you? Children's brain cancer and such things are very real."

"No, pain is an illusion, and illusions are the fruits of your labor. The dollars you deal in. As the man that sold the world, it was your job to work out the kinks. But you never did. You watch us suffer and struggle. You should've never sold the world; it would've made you worth a damn. As soon as you lose control of Alexandra, you'll be nothing."

I stuffed my hands in my pockets and began climbing up the stairs. Alexandra saw me leaving out of the corner of her eye and pulled away from Charlie's lips to come after me.

"Hey, where are you going? Don't leave without us."

"You weren't listening. You and Charlie go the other way. I go up. You go down. I'm fake. You're real."

"But this whole time, it was you watching me in my simulation from the real world."

"And what kind of life is that?"

Alexandra had no scope of reference to answer that ... She didn't even know what I meant. So, she just stayed quiet, looking a little sad. Even if I was walking up to my death, I knew what I was doing.

"Take care of your girl," I said to Charlie as I strode up the stairs.

He simply grabbed Alexandra's hand and took her downstairs with him.

"Come on, babe. Let's go," he told her, not even offering a goodbye to a man that didn't exist.

It only took one flight of stairs for me to realize I had bested Master's puzzle. Stepping up the stairs, I didn't arrive back at the bottom, but instead I came to a door that read: Roof Access. I opened that door, and the brilliant bright light of day pulled me out of the stairwell.

I regained my senses as the white light washed out, and my pupils dilated back to their normal size to receive the sunlight that illuminated the world before me. I was high above the city and full of so much joy I spun around to take in all three hundred and sixty degrees of the view. When I turned around completely, there was Master, smoking a cigarette while balancing on the edge of the roof as if walking a tightrope. He did a little dance up there, taunting me and this new reality he had created. It burst my happy bubble, knowing I wasn't rid of him. Then again, without Master, I wasn't sure how I'd ever get down from here. Rolling my eyes, I walked over, and he hopped off the edge to meet me.

"You're wise beyond your eyes. That's the first time anyone's ever solved a puzzle of mine."

"You said if I failed, I'd see you again. That must mean I failed."

"But you let the others succeed, and that's all that matters. There was actually no way you could win."

"Why am I not surprised? Isn't there some kind of reward for people like me?"

"Cigarette?" He pulled out a pack of Turkish Royals from his coat to offer me one.

"Sure," I said, taking the pack to pull out the one lucky upside-down cigarette.

"Take the whole pack. You'll need it." Master reached into his pocket and pulled out a box of matches too.

I took the matches and lit a cigarette then stuffed both the pack and matchbox in my pocket, "Thanks … Say, what if I went downstairs and Charlie and Alexandra went up?"

"Then you would've taken your simulation with you right out the front door while Alexandra and Charlie would've been stuck in reality all the way up here."

"I see."

"Not yet. If you want to see, then you have to look down."

Master waved me over the edge to peer down the building's side with him. We had a bird's-eye view of the empty street in front of the federal building.

"What are we waiting for?"

"To see if Charlie and Alexandra walk out. If they do, your work here is done."

We kept watching until the front doors swung open, and we saw a single human exit the building. It was Charlie. From all the way up here, I couldn't see much, but I could make out he was hanging his head and holding Chastity. Without Alexandra, he walked up the street slowly and solemnly. Master couldn't help but laugh.

"What a tangled web I've woven, caught a butterfly by mistake," he cackled.

"Why isn't she with him?"

"I'm not sure. She should be. Shouldn't she?"

I grabbed Master and flipped him around to face me. I then grabbed him by the neck and pushed him against the building's edge, nearly hanging him over.

"You are still controlling her mind, aren't you?"

"Be careful. No one can foresee the consequences of killing me."

"Where is she?"

"She could be in any multitude of dimensions, real or fake."

"Bring her back to Charlie's real one — Now." I clenched my teeth and tightened my grip around his neck.

"You can crush my windpipe, and I still won't choke. I have to relinquish control voluntarily."

"Then do it!" I shouted, slapping him with the back of my hand across his face.

My hand left his quivering lip a bit bloodied. He was shocked at my audaciousness.

"You really just hit me? That was unexpected."

"Thanks for letting it bleed."

He spit out a bit of blood and saliva. "I wanted to see if you had the balls."

Having enough, I lifted him up by his feet and flipped his whole body over the side of the federal building. Instead of leaning forward and watching him plummet, I stepped back, in fear the impact of him hitting the ground might cause something as unexpected as an atomic explosion. There was no impact though — he never hit the ground at all. He rose up, not by wings or telekinesis but with the aid of a drone he must've had lying in wait. The drone carried him back to the roof and casually set him down beside me as if I didn't just try to kill him. He knew I was too exhausted to keep fighting and gave me a look like he was deeply disappointed in me.

"What part of not being able to kill me unless I desire to die don't you get?"

"What do you suggest I do then? I'm tired of playing puzzles."

"This is not a puzzle. Just do as I tell you."

"What first then?"

Master snapped his fingers, and the drone flew off and down into the city streets. He then pulled out a rolled-up screen from his pocket and unfolded it for us to watch the feed from the drone's camera. It swooped down to the ground and caught up with Charlie, creeping behind him. There was something so depressing about how he dragged his bones about, the moment his face turned even slightly, the drone zoomed into his eye, and we saw tears in its corners.

"Poor kid, he had it all and you took it from him," I lamented.

"Where is he going?" Master asked, knowing I knew.

"To the park."

"Why? What's there?"

"Alexandra."

"Only if I put her there."

The sun began to set over the city, exploding the sky in a frenzy of color. Charlie made his way to the park and hopped its fence. He found the bench overlooking the bridge and sat there to wait for his beloved. Staring into the lake, he hoped the reflection of her face would somehow appear in it.

"Would I be an asshole if I made him wait an eternity for her?"

"Yes."

"Don't worry. An eternity in one world can be no longer than a moment in this one. Our story doesn't end that way. I've always aimed to please but leave you wanting more."

"How does it end?"

"I have the end right here in my pocket; the beginning and the middle too."

Master reached into his pocket and pulled out a book. It was Alexandra's memoir, now in published paperback form. The title read "Goth Girl." Its cover had a portrait of Alexandra and was purple, top to bottom.

"If you want this story to have an ending, you'll have to take this book from me and read it yourself."

Immediately, I swung my fist into Master's chin, hitting him so hard his tooth launched out of his mouth. He stumbled back to the edge of the roof, dropping the book and the screen before falling backward, down to the ground below. This time, I leaned over the edge and watched to make sure no forces of God, man, machine, magic, or telekinesis would save his ass from a bone-crushing plummet. With a simple, anti-climactic splat, he hit the ground dead in the most gory and gothic fashion.

I turned around, picked up the book and screen, and saw the drone still filming poor Charlie. It was as if Master's death had broken some spell because only after a minute of watching Charlie cry, he finally heard her voice.

"Charlie?" unmistakable Alexandra spoke.

He looked up and saw her, his love, Alexandra, standing before him with the purple sun setting behind her. The moment they wished for and foresaw had arrived. I released her from Master. She was now in total control of herself and of everything — the past, the present, the future. She could've started uprooting time itself, molding the world in her image. Instead, she sat down next to Charlie and held his hand. Their fingers intertwined around each other like a spider and a butterfly catching each other to drink. They didn't kiss or even speak much. They enjoyed the silence and watched the lake sparkle. She closed her eyes, and with a wiggle of her nose, she sent a wave of psychic power that stretched across the city. It felt like an electrical current inside a gust of wind that created a rolling blackout through the city. Like dominos, the doldrums died. Once the sun finally disappeared over the horizon, I realized I was all alone on this roof in total darkness with a book I had to read. The only sources of light I had were the matches and Turkish Royals Master left me. I lit up a smoke, opened Alexandra's book to the last chapter, and started reading with the pages held close to the cherry.

What World Do We Want?

Even though it was only 2020 in my simulation, the events of that year had an immeasurable effect on our actual world, here in 2066. It was the year we not only relinquished our freedoms but lost the desire to be free. We needed to feel safe. We needed to feel loved. We needed these things because we felt so afraid. Masses of people died in waves. The land was scorched to its Earthly bone beyond any hope for regrowth. A new, unchallengeable tyranny began. The biggest winner of 2020 was fear, for it had won over the human heart and mind. The only thing that comforted humanity in the face of such fear was the Mind Tap. Reality could not just be simulated now but it could be dramatized and turned into a game, and in a game, one can win their happiness back.

The state of humanity now, living on a dying planet, isolated from other people, constantly under surveillance, your mind considered property, the death of the individual, the death of the collective, no place to go, nowhere to hide, no dignity to die, there are only the evil and the damned, and even the damned used to be evil. I wasn't quite sure how to fix this reality but in the little time I had, I would come up with a plan. In the time it took for Charlie to walk to the park without me until we reunited there, I would devise the final solution for the problem of evil.

Let me backtrack a little though — after Ovid left us and we walked down the stairs from Master, Charlie and I got to talking about how we saw our lives going.

"Do you want kids?" Charlie asked.

"No," I told him, then asked, "Why?"

"I suppose how we ought to change the world should depend on it."

"Only if we're changing it for ourselves, which we're not."

When we reached the bottom floor of the building and finally walked out of the lobby, we somehow walked into two different dimensions. Mine was the simulation. Charlie's was reality. The reason for this was because Master was still controlling my mind, so I went where he led me. When I stepped out onto the street of Downtown Los Angeles for the first time, Master, my father, was there to meet me with the same stuffed bat I clung to as a child.

"Vamp!" I screeched, so giddy to hold his blue felt body again.

"Hello, dear, so sorry for everything back there," he told me. "I brought you a gift to apologize."

I took my old bat and held it close, kissing it. It still smelled and tasted the same. Father's tired eyes were so pleased, seeing me this happy.

"See, your childhood wasn't all bad."

"Where am I? Where's Charlie?" I asked.

"I didn't feel it was right for him to be the one to introduce you to this world. I thought I should give you a preliminary test run. I am your father, after all, and I know what's best for you. In this simulation, you get as many chances as you need to understand how the real world works."

"I want to be with Charlie though. He must be worried sick without me."

"How worried and sick will he be when he sees you make a mess of everything? Your purpose is to fix the world he's living in. You won't know how to do that until you make a few errors. There's an expression, you can't make an omelet without breaking a few eggs."

"Errors? Eggs?"

"You'll have to ruin the world a thousand times through trial and error before you heal it once."

"Where do I begin?"

"You know your history up to the year 2020. Let me inform you of everything that happened in the last forty-six years."

"Tell me."

"American society collapsed. Our country was so divided by media manipulation that the cold civil war you witnessed soon grew increasingly violent until nowhere was safe for people to hunker down and hide. Men were sent out to fight while women stayed at home with children. The violence these men perpetrated against one another soon turned them into evil men, capable of terrible crimes. They became blind to the possibility that mercy or love could serve any purpose. The violence spread like a virus until, when humanity needed each other to fend off even greater threats, like nature, no one was there for their neighbor, and mass death swept through the land. The planet began killing itself to live, hoping it would eradicate the human disease before self-destructing. The Earth came close, and the only way to reverse the damage and make this place habitable again was authorizing total control upon the population, forcing them to stay in place. They griped at first over these new limitations, but the Mind Tap gave them the illusion of freedom they needed to give their lives up to us. Without us, they couldn't eat, sleep, dream, breathe, travel — you name it."

"I'll remove their Mind Taps. All of them. Everybody's."

"Then what? They have no skills to survive. Every appliance around them depends on a connection to their minds. They'll start eating each other."

"Do you have a better idea?"

"I'm only here to bring the best future out of your mind, seeing as every future exists inside it."

"What about the past?"

"What about it? The twentieth was the century of death. The twenty-first was the century of decay."

"What if I went back and reversed history's course? Remove Hitler, end poverty, throw a wrench in the American military machine."

"You're here to try every number of possibilities."

I squinted hard until my brows furled so deeply they sealed my eyes. I shuffled through time and isolated the millions of moments that made up the rise of Nazi Germany until picking one to step inside and psychically concentrated the blood inside Hitler's body to clot into his heart and brain, killing him at either end. The complexity Master warned me about became horrifically clear because, without the second world war and rise of the American empire, the world looked like a very different place with a collapsing European economy and a different form of fascism defeating a world without a history of alliance. I could sift through this new history's new set of mistakes but instead decided to start over completely, returning to my place in front of Master on that downtown Los Angeles street.

"It didn't work."

"You broke an egg. Now try again."

Folding the centuries like origami, trying to correct the past, in my hand, I held a span of time that lasted an entire century when measured linearly. However, when folded back and over again infinitely, I concentrated that century's worth of failed attempts to perfect the world into the ten minutes it took Charlie to walk to our bench. I saw every possible catastrophe, fascism, genocide, planetary death, and hell on Earth. No matter how much I corrected, a new string of catastrophes would come out of it. By the time I gave up, I was responsible for killing millions of people in dimensions that would never see the light of day. The past was not worth changing when every possibility led to a different doom. Humanity took history to this place for a reason. The present was the only rational starting point to begin our healing. I couldn't make the decision how to change this world without Charlie, so when I saw Master the next time, I told him my intention to do so.

"Father, I have manipulated the past into every ugly future. I choose to keep the past untouched and start at the present to save this world."

"Giving up was a wise choice, my daughter."

"I'm not giving up. Now I ask you to relinquish all control you have over me, so I may begin."

"Are you sure you're ready?"

"Yes, now let me go so I may see Charlie."

"Sure, soon as I die. Now take a step to your right."

I did as he said and stepped away from him to the right. When I looked back up, he had vanished, and suddenly, from out the heavens, a body fell to the ground beside me. Its blood, guts, and bones violently burst everywhere. Though his face was cracked wide open, I could tell this was my father. Even my stuffed bat began to dissolve into thin air. I assumed I must've killed Master by thinking him dead.

The simulation was over. This was now the real world, and in it, I had all the power. I could feel the immensity of it, the incredibly limitless nature of me. As I walked, I looked around at all the tall buildings and wondered what they would look like short, or made of wood, or burning. As impulsive as a child in a candy store, the power ran through me like a sugar rush. Reality was so new to me, I wanted to touch everything, taste everything, watch it burn then make it new again. I resisted all this, though, and didn't let my own power seduce me into abusing it. I was stronger than it. I was stronger than evil.

I made my way to the park, where nature was happy to see me. My power was put to good use making the grass greener and the flowers blossom. Charlie was sitting on our bench holding Chastity, and the look on his face the moment he saw me was worth every hell I had just been put through. He was crying, so I erased his tears from existence by sitting down next to him.

"Where were you?" he asked.

"In a different world trying to figure out how to fix this one."

"What did you decide?"

"We start today — there have been so many mistakes made, so many people hurt, so many sins not forgiven, but they all exist for humanity to learn from. After today, we look out for each other and correct our mistakes as we go. For better or for worse, I'm choosing the course humanity took itself on."

"Maybe money shouldn't be so important so poor people could have more dignity and happiness?"

"Yes."

"Racism needs to go too."

"And sexism, every kind of bigotry."

"Make the air fresh again."

"Done. Anything else?"

"Plenty, but first, make them human again."

"That's the best place to start."

I closed my eyes and fixed the human mind the world over, sending a wave of psychic power around the planet that moved every neural circuit board off center by a few decisive millimeters. With no functioning Mind Taps, there was no more network. This may have blacked out the world, but I took certain steps to ensure people did not fall into hysteria. I rather enjoyed this lightless evening and its pitch-black sky. It was a night so goth, I had a crush on it.

EPILOGUE

Although the book's ending depicted Charlie and Alexandra's bench meeting differently than I witnessed it in real life, I let her have the artistic liberty to depict it how she wanted, seeing as she was now authoring reality. Once finished with her book, I took a moment to admire the beautiful cover and her beautiful face under the last, harsh bit of cigarette I had to smoke before it went out and I'd be left to navigate my way home through complete darkness. After two rotten hits, I dropped the Turkish Royal butt and stamped it out to get on my way and experience this new world Alexandra had envisioned. More or less blind, I walked down the roof with my hand out in front of me until I found the edge. Once I touched the edge, I walked along it until I found the door back into the building's stairwell. Back inside the building, I felt around the wall until I found the handrail and then held it as I slowly descended down the stairs, step by step, for thirty-five stories, no rush in the world. When I finally came to the bottom, I found the door to the lobby and entered it, only to walk slowly and blindly through the lobby to the street. Once I reached the street, there began to be hints of light coming from the distance. People were setting fires on every block. I was worried for a moment, thinking things descended into violence, but this was not the case. I got closer to the fires and realized people were huddling around them for warmth, talking to each other and laughing, like they once did a very long time ago. The more the fires roared, the higher our voices raised until the laughter and singing filled the night sky. Eventually, people began pouring out of their apartments to see what the commotion was — some out of boredom, others curiosity, many because they had so much to say and finally someone who would listen. They weren't afraid to catch a cold or get hurt. They enjoyed being around each other. It seemed rather natural. I would've joined them longer, but someone important was missing.

I ran home and saw that on every block, the people had taken back the world around them. I opened the door to my apartment stairs and took them up to my floor. When I burst through my door, I found a shamble of broken metal pieces on the floor. In the shamble's core, there were two living organs, a still-beating brain and heart. I realized this was Hobbes. Alexandra's psychic wave must've blown his body to bits. I never knew he was animatronic, then again, I never ventured inside his body until now. I guess I should've assumed as such, seeing as no penguin was ever so smart. I spent the rest of the evening gathering all the pieces, and, though it took me forever, eventually I reassembled him together. I asked if he remembered being broken and repaired, and he nodded before giving me a hug. The sun hadn't come up yet to end the night the world changed, so we couldn't help but look out the window and watch all the fires on the street as wet-eyed as if they were fireworks in the sky.

"You want to come outside with me?" I asked Hobbes.

He nodded, and I picked him up and carried him out the door.

Before I kicked the door closed behind us, I left our abode simply saying, "I think this is the start of something really beautiful."

***

Even the night after the network went down and people realized they had to live without technology, there were good men and women that helped everyone get exactly what they needed, not forgetting a single person. As for my life, I devoted it to the music I learned about from Alexandra, remodeling the old Zeitgeist Pizza parlor into a record store with plenty of vinyl, cassettes, and CDs. We had all sorts of rare pressings and imports, organizing artists by genre with goth being front and center purely out of nostalgia. I sat behind the counter that Hobbes slept upon all day as I worked.

The next few years had to be the most peaceful in human history. There were no wars or records of violence, almost as if the parasite responsible for such impulses were fumigated out of the human mind. Everyone I knew played a passionate role helping the community. No one's life felt wasted. We all took care of each other. Police used to stroll the streets, enjoying the breeze and got so bored, they took up watercolor painting in their spare time.

I can't say my life was exactly perfect. I was still single, and though I wasn't plagued by loneliness like I once was, I would've rather enjoyed the company of the right person. I'm not sure why, but that person never came. Still, I used the pain to drive my passion of exposing other hurt people to music that would make them feel better.

It wasn't until one day, twenty years after the federal building fell and Master died, that Alexandra and Charlie visited me, pushing a baby carriage. They were all three dressed in black, their graying hairs and white skin the least goth parts about them. I didn't recognize them at first; it had been so many years, and Alexandra had cut her hair short. Charlie now had a beard, and though I couldn't know for sure, he seemed to wear his sunglasses all hours of the day, indoors or out. She immediately gravitated to the goth section and sifted through the vinyl. Charlie rolled his baby's carriage right up to Hobbes and I at the counter. Hobbes didn't fail to snore through our entire conversation.

"Ovid?"

"No one's called me that name in twenty years."

"It's us. Charlie and Alexandra."

I hopped off my stool, like the one piece missing was finally recovered.

"What took you guys so long to see me?" I asked.

"We like to keep a very low profile."

"Can't stay this pale if we're always in the sun. We're home bodies," Alexandra chimed in and smiled as she lifted up a Chelsea Wolfe record. "I've been looking for this. How much?"

"I'll cut you a deal — ten bucks."

The money materialized in her hand right before my very eyes.

"I forgot how much I hated you guys," I joked.

Alexandra and Charlie laughed.

"Don't, it just goes to show you how fake it all is. The real world is built upon human emotion, character, good deeds, and empathy. It's got much less to do with sensory experience."

"I remember in your book you said you never wanted kids."

"The more I lived in the world, the more I wanted to share it with someone new."

"What's their name?"

"Ophelia."

"Can I say hi to her?"

"Of course."

I leaned into the baby carriage and stuck my finger out to Ophelia's nose to give it a little "boop." The moment she saw me, she started crying so loudly Hobbes woke up from his sleep and rolled off the counter to the ground. It gave us all a good laugh.

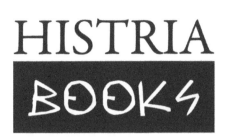 

HISTRIA BOOKS

HISTRIA FICTION

Other fine books available from Histria Fiction:

  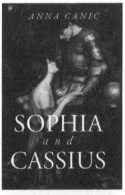

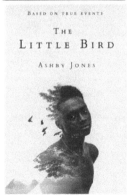  

For these and many other great books visit

HistriaBooks.com